Dr. Guillotine's Nightmare and Other Short Stories
by
Bob Little

ISBN 9780980027952

For more information contact
tersebob@gmail.com

Contents

Introduction

I like to have a little surprise at the end of my stories. Often this is a reverse of the situation for the bad guy. Sometimes it is just an unforeseen consequence. I like O'Henry (or should I say William Sidney Porter) for the twist at the end of each of his stories.

In two of the tales told in this book, I have represented real people, but have shown them in a fiction that explores possibilities. They are not real events. In both cases the historical facts are meager.

I have delighted in the writings of Ambrose Bierce. In writing about his disappearance in Mexico, I have tried to imagine how he would have written it. In many of my more recent stories I have drawn upon his imaginative and bizarre stories.

I've learned a lot from O'Henry and Bierce. I hope that the reader is entertained by what I have written.

Doctor Guillotine's Nightmare

The fear of the LORD is the beginning of knowledge: but fools despise wisdom and instruction. (Old Testament / Proverbs 1:7)

"My machine will take off a head in a twinkling and the victim will feel nothing but a refreshing coolness. We cannot make too much haste, gentlemen, to allow the nation to enjoy this advantage." Joseph Ignace Guillotine, Statement to the French Assembly, 1789.

It was the heart of the French revolution of 1793. Doctor Joseph Ignace Guillotine was musing in his study – speculating on the success of the marvelous beheading machine he had recommended. Heads were rolling off the guillotine daily as the royal and crown heads of France were toppling off the scaffold into buckets.

Was there much pain? The good doctor thought not. This was the whole purpose of the invention. The quick snap of the knife and the nerves were severed – the head sliced away. How convenient for the haughty royal family that the machine had come along when it did, and in one short gasp they were severed from life with so little hurt. It was practically painless. No more strangulation from a faulty hangman's noose. No more bungled chopping of the executioner's axe.

He swirled a little glass of wine in his hand. It was blood red. It dulled the senses and the conscience.

He dozed a little. His assistant would wake him when he returned. He lifted his head just as there was a knock at the door.

"The basket is very heavy!" It was Pierre fumbling at the door latch. "Please help me, Doctor!"

Slowly Joseph edged to the door. It was as though his feet were lead. His head was full of sleep. The wine had made everything blurry.

Just as he reached the door, Pierre succeeded in pushing in. His burden was thrust in front of the doctor. The contents of the basket leered up at him.

"These were all there were today."

The doctor stepped back. The scene before him was horrible. Pierre emptied the basket, methodically arranging each head on a shelf in the doctor's study. Joseph thought he remembered the shelf being filled with jars. Now it supported the lifeless heads of the executioner's "window". That was what the guillotine had come to be called. It looked a little like a window.

Once he finished, Pierre left the room and went out into the night. Doctor Guillotine looked around. On the shelf were the heads of Louis XVI, his queen, Marie Antoinette, and friends. All looked perfectly serene. There was no evidence of shock or pain.

Did they smile? For an instant it seemed so. That would prove his point and set his mind at ease. He would test them - check the tissue for any sign of life after decapitation. Perhaps he could determine if death was instant. He turned away to pick up his instruments.

"You said it would be painless." He thought Pierre spoke, but his assistant had left.

He faced the heads again. They were all the same but one. It was not a smile he saw but a leer. Joseph rubbed his eyes. The leer was still there.

"You lied, Doctor." He saw it clearly. The King's lips moved. How could that be?

His heart murmured. The King was alive. No, his head was alive. How could it be painless if his head was still alive?

Hesitantly, Joseph crept over to the shelf and peered at the King's head. He lifted the head onto his examining table. Fresh blood was on his hands. He wiped them on his apron.

Behind him another head spoke. "It hurts ever so much." It was Antoinette's voice, the Queen. He lowered his eyes. She screamed.

One by one the heads addressed him. The King was the last to speak: "You have failed all France, Joseph Guillotine. Now you will suffer as we."

There was a knock at the door. The doctor swept the King's head into the basket again. He cleared the shelf of the rest of the heads. One bit him on the arm as he did so. All went back into the basket. He grasped his bleeding arm. Only then did he answer the door.

"Citizen Guillotine?" Two men in uniforms sporting the tricolor stood waiting. "We have orders from the committee to arrest you."

Joseph was dumbfounded. He knew what was going to happen. He knew it would not be painless. He struggled.

A glass crashed to the floor. He was alone. It was only a dream. Then there was a knock at the door. He opened it. There stood two men in uniforms. They wore the popular tricolor.

Historical Notes

Doctor Guillotine did not invent the beheading machine. He recommended this humane means of execution, but did not believe in capital punishment.

Another Doctor Guillotine was executed by the guillotine during the revolution, but his initials were J. M.

As the Reign of Terror drew to a close, Doctor Joseph-Ignace Guillotine was arrested; however, he was released in 1794 with his head still on his shoulders.

The Ironic Fate of Ambrose Bierce

Discretion shall preserve thee, understanding shall keep thee: (Old Testament / Proverbs 2:11)

"How appropriate!" Ambrose thought to himself, "If I'm not rescued, I will most certainly die in a cemetery." Indeed, the courageous veteran of the civil war who suffered a severe head wound during that altercation, the teller of gruesome tales of that great atrocity and numerous twisted events concerning terror and death was very near his own last hour on earth.

At least there would be a large assembly for his demise. That was something he hadn't planned. Everyone from the town of Sierra Mojada was present for the occasion. The populous was held behind a low wall surrounding the austere camp of the dead by a small army of soldiers serving the self appointed president of Mexico.

Dust rose in clouds as the crowd stomped and kicked about between the green less burial mounds. Ambrose coughed. He could hardly breathe, something that had troubled him ever since that fateful day when he was wounded at the Battle of Kennesaw Mountain.

Younger citizens jumped up and down to get a better view of the carnage and by doing so increased the dust and commotion. The darling of the community dressed in a white blouse and red skirt smiled on the soldiers holding back the crowd and they stepped aside to let her through. She sauntered up to the accused and removed a bright red scarf from her neck and entwined it lovingly about the neck of the helpless man at the wall. She kissed him softly and returned to her people who nodded their approval.

A young priest drew near the condemned man. Ambrose shook his head, refusing last rights. The cleric backed away, crossed himself and stood to one side.

Up the acclivity upon which the town of Sierra Mojada stood, Ambrose believed he could see Valdez standing attentively by a tree, waiting to rain down his corral of mules to interrupt the action. Behind the fat man were green trees and white-washed houses bathed in the sun and climbing up the hill to the foot of the steep mountains behind.

Ambrose was dressed more like a mortician than a retired writer. He made an impressive picture in his black suit and white hair. The army let him keep his black ebony cane because he looked a little unsteady.

The town militia stood before him - their uniforms consisted of bandoleers and blue scarves They formed a ragged row. Each man proudly shouldered a heavy musket.

Their captain, dressed in the official uniform of the Huerta Army trooped the line, swaggering as he pushed them about like toy soldiers. He tugged at an arm here and there until the guns were all at a similar angle. His duty with the town soldiers was distasteful. He had dreams of serving his country in the field of conflict. He would make good his contribution here and hope for a better chance to excel.

Ambrose mused over the opportune timing of his pending finale. He had predicted the event, telling his public in the United States that he would appreciate death as a spy at the hands of a firing squad much more than falling down a cellar stair. He had boldly come to Mexico hoping for an encounter with death in the roil of the revolution that swallowed the nation.

Nevertheless, his present state of affairs came as a surprise. How did he get here so soon and so flawlessly? Just yesterday he was eager to join Pancho Villa in Ojinaga. Villa was winning his way through northern Mexico with exciting success. Town after town fell to his superior forces. As governor of the state of Chihuahua he had taken advantage of his privilege as commanding general of the State forces to go to war against the federal government. Now he was the fly in the middle of President Huerta's pie.

It was just this morning that Ambrose had set out to join Villa and his army in the most eastern part of his domain. Villa had Federal forces trapped against the border with the United States opposite the Presidio in Texas and was pounding them to shreds.

When Ambrose woke up in Chihuahua City it was already ten o'clock in the morning. At 71 years old sleeping late had become a habit. He had no column to write and wasn't concerned with taking notes among the camp followers. The weather was pleasant and conducive to rest. He took a leisurely breakfast, washed and dressed. He didn't bother to shave. It wasn't necessary.

At the station he learned that the train for Ojinaga had left an hour before. He could speak the language well enough to make himself understood, but it was difficult to understand the harried station master. "What track was that?" he asked for the second time.

He found the right track and waited several hours for it to fill with cars. He wasn't sure that he had the right train until he saw that the passengers were mostly men anxious to go where the action was. "Were they all going to the fight?" he asked himself.

The cars were crowded. He pushed his way to a seat that had been missed and sat alone. No one was brave enough to share the seat with the tall stranger.

The windows were open or missing. Thick smoke mingled with earthen grime stirred by the train's progress filled his lungs during the ride. He had a small device for clearing his air passages and relieving the pain that often bothered his head from the wound that he had sustained during the war. He inhaled some of his "medicine" and settled down to endure the journey. He was soon dozing in spite of the press of passengers that filled the car. There were no dreams in the fog of his unconscious travail.

When the train stopped, a smelly mule skinner named Valdez rolled onto the seat beside him, upset his nap and introduced himself. He spoke fair English for a man of such humble circumstances.
"Where are you going, Señor?"

Although Ambrose prided himself on being precise, in this case, he decided to conceal his intentions. "To the border."

"All the way to the border?"

Bierce looked the man up and down. "Ah, yes, of course."

"I am going the same way, Señor. We must change trains at the next stop. If you like, I will see that you get on the right car."

"Change trains?"

"Yes, otherwise you could end up in Mexico City."

The mule skinner's suggestion puzzled Ambrose. Mexico City was south not east. How could a train going east end up in Mexico City? Ambrose looked out the window hoping to make some sense out of his environment. Where were they?

It wasn't long until the train stopped again. Ambrose followed the Mexican until they were seated on the new car. He was still drowsy and appreciated the help.

"I gather mules for the army," said Valdez. "They need lots of mules to carry supplies."

"Mules," Ambrose thought. "Something about mules was familiar to him."

Ah, yes: *Brigadier General Juniper Doke*, the story he had written about a fictitious Union general during the civil war. Doke was a witless political appointee who gathered mules together in case of a possible retreat by his men. If the occasion presented itself each man was to mount a mule and ride to safety. When the time came for retreat the mules broke loose and routed an entire Confederate army.

Ambrose recited the story to Valdez just to pass the time.

"That is a very interesting story, Señor. You should have it published."

"I have."

"Then you must be a famous writer. I hope you are not too famous. If any of the generals had read your story they might have me shot as a spy-me having all these mules."

"I suppose you have to be careful about such things."

"Oh, yes, Señor. Without that story, they would never suspect a poor mule skinner of having such power."

"The generals want all the power to themselves."

"Si, Señor." From this point on Valdez became silent. Perhaps he was thinking of the possibilities for a poor mule skinner.

Ambrose was pondering the same idea. What if he were to assemble a thousand or more of these mules? He could chase them into an army and drive the troops to distraction – maybe even drive them into the hills. Maybe Valdez was thinking of doing just that. What if he was one of Huerta's men.

"How many of these mules have you gathered?"

"Oh, at least a thousand. They are in a corral up in the hills. If I wanted to destroy an army, I could drive them down in an instant."

"I suppose that one could do this best when the army was concentrated in the plaza or something similar?"

"If I intended to do such a thing I would have one of my men catch them when they were all in a small area; then I would have him give some signal like several shots in a row; but that is just what you call speculation."

"You would never do such a thing?"

[11]

"Oh, no, Señor. I would lose all my mules. I am making lots of money from the army. Why would I do such a thing?"

The two men became silent once more. Ambrose slept. Valdez gazed into the crowd around him wondering if anyone understood what they had discussed. He knew that he was already a marked man if anyone reported that he had spoken to an American. Americans were suspect. Everyone knew that Americans were in favor of their enemy.

Not much chance of his being reported. Those on the train were mostly miners looking for work in La Esmeralda. There was a slim chance that there was a spy among them.

The train meandered through the mountains and over the plains. It seemed to turn on itself and then came to a siding in a small train station.

"This is La Esmeralda!" Valdez proclaimed as the train rolled to a stop. "It's a mining town. Most of those on the train are here to work in the mine." The occupation of the men came as a surprise to Ambrose.

"I'll be going up the hill from here to report to the army. You will stay on the train. It goes right to the border."

"So the army is here."Ambrose thought. Since Valdez was going to the army and had a vested interest in helping with his mules, Ambrose decided to change his story. "Actually, I think I'll be going along with you. I have an assignment with the army too."

"You're not going to the border then?"

"No, since you are helping the army, I can tell you the truth."

"An American with the army! You must be a very important man, Señor?

"Hardly. I'm only a humble writer."

"A correspondent then?" Valdez led the way up the hill.

"Not really. Just an observer."

As they reached the outskirts of the town on the hill Ambrose asked: "I thought there would still be fighting."

"You are misinformed, Señor. There is no fighting here. The army is in complete control of the city."

"Where can I find the general's staff?"

"You will find the officers in the big mansion on the plaza. I am going there myself."

The two men drew the attention of the townsmen as they walked side by side to the general's mansion. When they arrived, the mule skinner introduced Ambrose as a famous American writer and then reported the mules he had ready now to carry supplies.

"Where is General Villa?" Ambrose blurted out in his simple Spanish.

"Not here I hope," said one of the clerks. "We have had no reports of his whereabouts since this morning when he overthrew Ojinaga."

"Then the battle is over."

"Yes, Señor."

"You don't know where I can find him then?"

"No, we would like to know ourselves, but why are you interested in his whereabouts?"

"I just thought he would be here."

"Here – General Pancho Villa here?"

"Yes, I would like to talk to him. Are you sure you don't know where he is?"

One of the officers standing by interrupted. "You want to talk to General Villa?"

"Yes, are you refusing to let me see him?"

"Wait here a minute!" The officer left the outer office and entered a room to one side marked 'Private'. He emerged again with another officer, one with a lot of gold braid.

"You say you want to talk to Villa?" The braided officer asked.

"Yes, where is he. I need to see him."

The two officers looked at each other quizzically. The commander – at least that seemed what he was – whispered something to the other officer, and he went over to the clerk and whispered something to him, and the clerk ran out of the office and returned with two other men.

"You will go with these men, Señor," said the commander.

"Will I get to see General Villa?"

"No doubt you will see him once we catch up with him." Ambrose was puzzled by the officer's remark. Into what kind of fool's game had he fallen?

Instead of taking Ambrose to General Villa the two soldiers took him to the town jail.

At midnight, Ambrose had a visitor. It was dark and he could hardly recognize the man who came to his cell.

"Where am I?"Ambrose asked.

"You are in jail, Señor." It was Valdez the mule skinner.

"Why?"

"You asked the wrong question."

"I simply wanted to see General Villa."

"Shhh! Don't use that name so freely. Only the jailer knows I am here and I wouldn't want it to get around that I visited the Yankee spy."

"Spy? They think I am a spy?"

"Yes, Señor. Where did you think you were?"

"In Ojinaga."

"You are not in Ojinaga. You are in Sierra Mojada 150 miles away from where you think you are. You are in the wrong town with the wrong army looking for the wrong general. Sierra Mojada is in the hands of Huerta's men.

"General Villa took Ojinaga this morning. Huerta's men are not happy with that. They think you are a spy. I don't think you are a spy. A spy would not be so obvious; you must be a very confused gringo."

"What are they going to do with me?"

"They will discuss that tomorrow."

"Do you think they will let me go?"

"I doubt it. Spies usually get shot. I like you, Señor. I don't want you to get shot. It is a bad idea, but I know a way that I can get you free."

"You can get me free?"

"Yes. If they decide to shoot you I will turn my mules loose and drive the army into the hills. Don't let them blind fold you. They will bind you hands but probably not your feet. When you hear shots run around behind the wall and hide. My mules will run them down and you can escape."

"Won't that be dangerous? Suppose they catch you?"

"They will probably be too busy."

Ambrose reflected on the possibility that Valdez might not succeed. It didn't matter. Either way he could not lose. If he got shot, so be it. If not, he could go to South America.

Bright and early the next day Ambrose was led to the cemetery and stood against a wall. The fancily dressed Captain moved the red scarf from Ambrose's neck to a button over the "spy's" heart. The pretty girl and the ladies wept.

"Listos - Apunten - Fuego," The captain barked. The sound of the guns was dreadfully loud. A woman screamed.

Ambrose coughed. Smoke swirled around him. His chest ached for oxygen. It was too much; his legs gave way and he slumped to the ground.

Miraculously, his head was clear – clearer than it had ever been before. He could breathe freely. He laughed. He guessed that they had missed.

He felt as though he were a new man. Swiftly he drifted around behind the wall. Valdez was there hiding. In his mind, the earth seemed to shake. Were those shouts of alarm he heard? Did he hear a thousand mules thundering down upon the militia, the peasants, and the army with its generals as they ran? Were they running in every direction? Was it a general route?

No, something was wrong. Wouldn't Valdez be driving his mules? Why would he be hiding here beside him? Everything began to blur as though he were in a dream.

On the hill near the town a fat man swung gently in the breeze from a tree - his arms tied behind him, his head drooped on his chest. One by one the army and the citizens of Sierra Mojada filed out of the cemetery and up the hill.

A young soldier picked up an ebony cane and used it to lift the limp head of the man by the wall. There was a smile on the face of the spy dressed in black.

"He is dead, Capitan! Just like that traitor, Valdez."

Brief Note on Ambrose Bierce

Ambrose Bierce, a retired writer disappears into Mexico in 1913 to join Pancho Villa and to observe the revolution. He wrote a letter from Chihuahua City in that same year. Nothing more was heard of him; however, a tall American was arrested and shot as a spy when he asked for Pancho Villa in the town of Sierra Mojada which was held by Villa's enemies. I am indebted to Leon Day and James Lienert for the idea for this story.

The Carpetbagger's Regret

*For her house inclineth unto death, and her paths unto the dead. None
that go unto her return again, neither take they hold of the paths of life.
(Old Testament / Proverbs 2:18 - 19)*

Aloysius stood on his tippy toes - mud all the way
up to his Yankee nose. He could see all the way across the
rice field to the mansion house where Miss Beauregard
Smith lived. A bee buzzed around his eyes looking for
something to land on.

Had he misjudged the girl? Nancy Louise
Beauregard Smith was a beautiful young belle of the old
south. Aloysius Leroy Peabody intended to make her his
wife. He had just become the district commissioner of
Beauregard County, but he intended to become the
governor of South Carolina.

He knew that he needed a good wife. A southern
belle would almost assure his success. He had been too
young to fight in what Nancy called the War Between the
States and so there was no tarnish on his character. He liked
the southerners. He respected their rights and his father
knew he would make a good commissioner.

Nancy's father was dead and it was assumed that
her two older brothers were also since they had not returned
after the war. Aloysius felt pretty secure. Nancy would
need someone like him to see that her honor was not
compromised.

They met at the Georgetown charity ball shortly
after he had arrived from New York. He liked her
immediately and saved her from two or three roughnecks
who tried to assert their rights as southern gentlemen.
Nancy was polite and let Aloysius know right away that she
and he mustn't be seen together too much as gossip would

destroy her reputation very quickly. The southerners didn't cotton to strangers from the north.

When Aloysius told her that he wanted to court her, she suggested caution. Perhaps he could come courting on the back side of the plantation so as not to encourage talk. He should go along the old Barlow road and turn at the stake on the west side of the property. She said that there was a road there that led directly to the house. The road was underwater at this season but if he turned at the stake and drove directly to the house he would have no problem.

He picked a Sunday morning when most folks would be at church and told her to expect him at noon. It was a short drive to the turn off – a pleasant February day.

Aloysius dressed in his best. He had polished his buggy and all of the harness. He had rubbed his horse to a beautiful shinny gloss. It was sure to impress Nancy.

Trees lined the main road and hid the rice field from view. He almost missed the turn off. No one would see him enter the plantation. He found the stake and left the thoroughfare turning in to the water covered field. The road Nancy described was well below the water surface. How far? Did he turn at the right place? Did he go on the right side of the stake? He must have made a mistake – one that caused him deep concern.

The horse had not pulled him far into the field when the buggy slowed to a crawl. Then it stopped. Pull as he might the horse could not budge. They were stuck.

Aloysius drew his whip and beat the horse. The horse struggled. The more the horse struggled the more he sunk in the soft ooze. The buggy was soon up to the axles. Aloysius looked around. Perhaps he should abandon the buggy and go for help. What did he do wrong?

As he watched the horse struggle and sink, he decided that it would be foolish to leave the buggy. He would sink just as the horse was sinking. They would stop sinking when the buggy reached bottom.

Soon the buggy was immersed in the mud up to the seat. All that was left of the horse was his head and nose sticking out of the mud.

Aloysius stood. He stepped up on the seat. The buggy was soon out of sight. He was up to his waist in the mud and water.

His legs were giving out. He couldn't keep this up very much longer. He panicked. He called out, but there was no one to hear him. Was Nancy watching from the house? She knew he was coming. Then he saw her on the veranda. Was she waving? Maybe she was sending help.

He must have turned at the wrong spot. Surely Nancy would never have directed him wrong. Then again, maybe there was no road. Maybe she wanted to get rid of him. Were those the young bucks from the ball standing beside her on the veranda?

His cries for help floated on the air without avail. The soft oozy mud crept up past his chin. It enveloped his face and filled his nostrils, but no one came. His chest grew tight as the suffocating ooze seeped down into his system. All went black.

Then suddenly, he shot up, free of the mud. Curiously, he looked down on the top of his head as mud enveloped his slick brown hair. There were bubbles. He realized that his beautiful buggy, his horse and his virile body were buried beneath the South Carolina mud.

Aloysius surveyed the field, the mansion and those on the veranda. He was soaring above the field at tremendous speed – looking here and there, knowing the painful truth. He could clearly see the stake now at the edge of the field. In red letters, not visible to a man in a hurry, who was anxious to see his true love, were the words: "Danger, bottomless mud hole."

Timothy's Eagle

Envy thou not the oppressor, and choose none of his ways. (Old Testament / Proverbs 3:31)

Timothy was the toe-headed fourth son of a poor family in the ancient city of Brightland in the very north of the British Isles. Today we know this region as Scotland.

Timothy was crippled from birth. At first he could barely walk but in time he got about fairly well. In spite of his handicap, Timothy was a happy lad who enjoyed the outdoors.

Even though Horace, his father, was a brilliant physician he could do nothing that would heal Timothy. Perhaps this was the reason the family was so poor. Horace spent all he had trying different procedures to heal Timothy.

Judge Ophir the benevolent, was the chief judge of Brightland. In times past the people of Brightland had formed laws and chose a chief judge who would exercise those laws and protect his people. Under the Judges the people prospered. Through their industry and hard work their land became the envy of all the country round about. People flocked to Brightland to enjoy the blessings of this great nation.

Arthur was the younger brother of Judge Ophir. He went to the southernmost part of the island we know today as England and attempted to duplicate the government of his homeland. It was he that formed the famous Knights of the Round Table.

Timothy's father Horace was a very fine physician. Merlin of King Arthur's realm attempted to duplicate Horace's methods, but turned to magic when he failed. Had Judge Ophir known about Horace's talent he surely would have made him his chief physician.

Judge Ophir was a very religious man. Instead of Knights of the Round Table he had twelve religious advisors. All of them were good men except for Razman the Righteous. He called himself righteous.

Razman wanted to destroy the nation and make himself king. He sought every means to disrupt the government and to deride Judge Ophir.

Razman liked to hunt. He had two hawks that ferreted out game for him and then he would shoot them with his arrows.

His greatest hope was to kill an eagle. One day his hawks worried a great eagle away from its perch atop the heights in Brightland.

When the eagle swooped down to fight off the hawks, Razman shot an arrow and wounded it. The eagle fell to the earth but Razman could not find it; however, the eagle spotted Razman and never forgot his enemy.

Timothy happened to be in that area and marked the place where the eagle had landed. He limped to its hiding place and after soothing its frantic attempts to escape, took it home to his father.

Timothy told his father that he had found another creature that was lame like him and asked his father to help him heal the bird.

Horace examined the eagle and found that it had a broken wing. He splinted the wing. Timothy caught wild game with a snare and brought it to the eagle from day to day until the wing had mended.

One day Horace told Timothy that the eagle was no longer like him. He took pleasure in the healing of the eagle but was afraid that the boy would lose his friend now that he was healed.

As the eagle soared to great heights the boy rejoiced and marveled at his father's work. The boy called the eagle Boldwing. Boldwing did not fly away. Instead he returned to perch on the boy's shoulder.

Boldwing became a great help to Timothy's family. He and Timothy hunted each day and brought back much game so that Horace and his family prospered.

One day while Boldwing and Timothy were hunting, the eagle suddenly let out a piercing cry. He had spotted Razman his enemy in a thicket talking to highwaymen. As Boldwing circled the grove Timothy crept to the spot, hoping to bag some good game.

As Timothy cautiously parted the bushes that surrounded the thicket, he saw three men with Razman. Razman was instructing the men to spread rumors about Ophir's saying that he was corrupt and to strike down the Judge while he was in his garden praying.

Timothy hurried home on his gimpy legs and told his father. Horace could not believe that Razman the Righteous would do such a thing. He soon forgot his son's experience, but Timothy never did.

This year a great competition was to take place in which the winner would receive a great prize. The prize was to be 100 gold coins. It was a hunting contest. The entire nation was invited to come. Razman and his hawks were favored to win.

Timothy begged his father to let him compete. Boldwing was strong and practiced and Timothy knew he could do better than Razman and his hawks. With reluctance his father consented.

Razman thought the contest would be a good time to eliminate the Judge and take over the nation. He trained his hawks to attack the Judge by using a garment that only Ophir would wear.

On the day of the competition almost no one could beat Razman and his two hawks. At last the final competition came. Razman and Timothy were pitted against one another. Razman was confident that he could win the competition and kill the Judge during the festivities afterward.

At the signal, Razman released his two hawks and Timothy released his eagle. A rabbit was released and everyone cheered.

Razman directed his hawks to attack Boldwing, but the eagle was ready for them. He evaded them and captured the rabbit and dropped it at Timothy's feet.

Razman was livid. He accused Timothy of cheating. He said that an eagle was not the customary bird to use in a hunt.

There was great confusion while the people discussed this point. It was decided that an eagle was much the same as a hawk in the competition. Timothy had won.

Still more enraged, Razman signaled his hawks to attack Judge Ophir but the eagle worried the hawks away.

Frustrated in his attempt, Razman accused Timothy and his father of plotting against Ophir. He said that the eagle was trained to attack the Judge and that the hawks were trying to protect him.

He directed guards to arrest Horace and his son, but as they came to do so, Boldwing swooped down and sat upon Timothy's head, warding off the efforts of the officers.

But Horace was captured. When Horace was brought before Ophir he remembered what Timothy had said about the plot to kill the Judge and told the story that Timothy had told him.

Exposed for what he was, Razman drew a long knife and the Judge realized Razman's true purpose. He ordered his guards to take Razman but Razman had passed a law that no one should have a knife but him. The guards were afraid to approach Razman.

Boldwing left his perch on Timothy's head, and grabbing Razman by each shoulder with his sharp talons, lifted the evil man into the air and flew him to the farthest corner of the nation. He dropped him in a secluded valley surrounded by high mountains.

Judge Ophir awarded the 100 gold coins to Timothy. Timothy exclaimed that they need no longer be poor.

When Ophir heard the story of how Horace had healed the eagle and discovered this talent, he appointed him his chief physician.

Timothy was named Timothy the Terrible for his great hunting skills and he and Boldwing continued to hunt wild game in the lowlands of Brightland for many happy years.

The Odessa

Enter not into the path of the wicked, and go not in the way of evil men. Avoid it, pass not by it, turn from it, and pass away. For they sleep not, except they have done mischief; and their sleep is taken away, unless they cause some to fall. For they eat the bread of wickedness, and drink the wine of violence. (Old Testament / Proverbs 4:14 - 17)

Charles was just a sausage maker until the Odessa family came to St. Augustine. They were great customers. When his supply of meat ran out they agreed to supply the meat if he would only make the sausages.

Others in the small town began to prosper as well. Harry Odessa promised great changes in the community and he found ways to keep his promise. Harry spoke with great enthusiasm and eloquence. He was soon elected to the city council.

His methods were in sharp contrast to the laissez faire conservatives who sat alongside him in meeting. Undaunted, Harry lead the council out of the dark ages. He was popular with the youth. His guarantee of change was welcome among them.

No one noticed that several old families in the town disappeared shortly after the Odessa family came. Vacant homes and farms were appropriated by the Odessas. With fewer families to trade there was more business for those who remained. However the reduction of consumers and tax payers began to work a burden on the town.

When revenues and profits became low, Harry came to the rescue with loans and government subsidies. Lotteries promised income to the city and hope for the needy.

The townsmen thought that their troubles were at an end. Charles was ever foremost in cheering on the Odessa wave as it swept through the town. Harry Odessa was constant in his praise of his own programs.

Then, the older members of the township began to notice the disappearance of their neighbors. What had become of the old timers? The oldies complained that something was wrong. Why had so many of their dear friends disappeared? It was suggested that they were evil and had packed up in the night and left because of the goodness of the Odessa family.

This did not set well with the oldies and even some of the prominent business members of the community. Some resented the change. They wanted the old lazy fare conservative town that used to be.

About this time Charles found human teeth in the meat that was delivered to him by the Odessa family. He complained to Harry Odessa. Shortly afterward he disappeared.

The Odessa family took over his business. No one missed Charles much. He had always been a loud mouth and a braggart. It was assumed that he had cheated the Odessa family and slipped out of town unawares.

More people disappeared over the next few months. City taxes were raised to compensate and some businesses received government subsidies with the agreement that they would let their efforts be directly supervised by the Odessa family.

Then one day a terrible thing happened. A pestilence erupted in the town. Some said it was carried in the sausages that were produced by the Odessa family. The sausages were examined by a noted professor from an adjoining town. It was discovered that the sausages were made up of human flesh. They were indeed contaminated.

Before any court could try the Odessa, the family contracted this deadly disease and were all found dead.

The Death of the Golden Goose

Trust in the LORD with all thine heart; and lean not unto thine own understanding. In all thy ways acknowledge him, and he shall direct thy paths. (Old Testament / Proverbs 3:5 - 6)

Janice and Janet were twins. I have known them since high school. They were identical in every way except one. Janice was frugal and precise and Janet was generous and freewheeling.

They were lovely girls – both blond and blue eyed. Perhaps they were a little skinny, but let's just say well proportioned.

They delighted in confusing the boys they dated. When it suited them they even swapped dispositions. Janice would be generous and freewheeling and Janet would be frugal. I don't think she could be precise.

In spite of that, they never fooled me for long. I liked Janet. In fact I had a crush on her. In time, the crush gave way to romance and we thought about marriage, but it never happened.

I joined the Marines and along came Skylar Thomas. Skylar had served a hitch in the Navy. Janet and he met on his last leave before mustering out.

He impressed Janet with his uniform and all his ribbons. He was an ensign, I believe, and I was quickly forgotten.

In time she grew tired of Skylar and decided that married life was not for her. They divorced and she went away to an art school and in a very short time became a popular artist.

Her sister, Janice, married Skylar on the rebound. Janice studied law and became a fairly good attorney. At the time of her death, she was Assistant District Attorney for the city of Camptown.

I was shocked to read of her death in the Camptown Chronicle. It was reported as a water skiing accident, but there were circumstances reported that did not seem plausible. I talked it over with my editor, Tom Handly, and was soon on my way to Camptown with an assignment to do a piece on Janice and her untimely death. She was just forty years old.

Camptown was a small community that had masqueraded under several different names during its long history. In the 1850's it briefly went by the name of Prospect. Then as it filled with miners, it became Newfield. When the vein ran out, it came to be known as Lakeview. Then along came a speculator who promoted the name of Camptown. It became a Mecca for horse lovers and a private resort for rich celebrities. Nestled in the hills, it was isolated from the world around it. It was popular for its fast horses and beautiful women.

Janice and Janet were born there. I was born in nearby Rocky Creek. The little community of Rocky Creek was "the other side of the tracks" for Camptown residents. I never missed Rocky Creek, but driving into Camptown was like coming home.

Janet had come home the year before. She roamed the hills breathing in the mountain air and producing some of the finest landscapes of her career. The New York market was buying them up as fast as she could paint them.

Ask me how I know. I've never forgotten Janet and have never missed one of her shows.

We write once in a while or I should say I do. Janet sends a card now and then. Sometimes, she sends me a brief e-mail, but she hasn't responded since the death of her sister.

The biggest thing that caused me to question Janice's accident was that she was cremated almost the very next day. I was sure Janet would report on that. She didn't. She didn't even thank me for the flowers I wired her.

A whole month had passed. I was surprised that I could convince the boss that the tragedy was still news. However, I billed Janice as a wealthy heiress. As far as I knew, the family fortune would go to her estate. Janet was too frivolous to control any of the wealth. She told me she had only a meager trust fund.

I was sure that Skylar would get the whole pot. It was even possible that he contrived his wife's death just to pick up the estate. However, he hardly had the smarts to carry out such an operation.

He really wasn't very bright and he couldn't leave the races alone. He told Janice he was a professional gambler. A gambler he was. A professional he was not. Janet told me he threw money away as fast as Janice made it. His gambling debts amounted to several thousand dollars a month. I think Janet was helping Janice meet the bills.

Skylar's problem put both he and Janice in a dangerous position. It was rumored that Camptown had its own gambling syndicate although no one liked to talk about it. I understand that pressure for repayment got pretty heavy after a few months.

Janice had prosecuted several collectors who had pushed a little too hard over the last four years. Several people were beaten severely. When they reported to the hospital, Janice was summoned. She knew just who to charge. Janice's death could have been the result of Skylar's gambling or her effort to stop brutal enforcers. The accident might have been planned and carried out by the syndicate.

After checking in at the Starting Gate – a motel near the track, I drove over to the Coroner's office. "There was nothing unusual about Janice's death," said the Deputy Coroner. "Her head was split wide open when she hit the rocks on the east side of the lake."

"Who saw the accident? I asked.

"Her husband and her sister."

"They were the only ones on the lake?"

"It was a week day. People only use the lake on weekends now."

I examined the Coroner's report for any clue to foul play. It seemed odd to me that only Skylar and Janet were there to witness the accident. It also bothered me that Janice was in the water alone. I knew that she didn't like water skiing. Janet was the expert. She would be in the water before Janice, but the report said both Skylar and Janet were in the boat.

I decided that once I had a shower and settled in I would call Janet and ask for an interview. She certainly could not refuse an old friend. She might even need a little cheering up and she loved to party.

I still hadn't dressed when I called her. Skylar answered. "What do you want?" he barked.

"Let me talk to Janet."

"She isn't talking to anyone. Call back in a month." He hung up with that and I was left standing there bewildered in my skivvies.

I was sure Janet would talk to me if she knew I was calling. I'd have to find a way to talk to Janet when Skylar wasn't around.

There was a barber shop around the corner from the Starting Gate. I could use a trim and I knew the barber. Johnny Newsom filled me in on all the gossip around town including some of the things I really wanted to know. It turned out that Janice's daughter was in town and she'd received the same treatment from Skylar that I had.

She was furious because Skylar held a memorial for her mother before she was even notified. Why didn't Skylar notify her? Something very suspicious had happened in Camptown - something that I intended to uncover.

I decided that if I couldn't talk to Janet I would do the next best thing. Janet's Aunt Jasmine lived nearby. Perhaps she could give me a few pointers.

Jasmine was a wild and racy girl in her day. She doted on Janet because they both viewed the world from the same angle. I was soon knocking on her door

"Matt! It's been a long time since I've seen you. Come right in!"

"I'll only stay a minute, Jasmine. I just wanted to ask you some questions."

"Nonsense. You know I always liked you. Stay as long as you like. I'd enjoy your company. It's too bad you and Janet never married. I should have liked having you in the Jalesco family.

"Thank you, Jasmine."

"I suppose you've seen my famous niece already. Isn't it amazing how she's made a success of herself? She didn't need the family millions to do it either."

"It is amazing?" I admitted. "I haven't seen her. In fact, I can't get past Skylar. Have you had a chance to talk to her since Janice died?"

"It's peculiar, Matt. She won't see me either. The last time we talked was a week before the accident."

"That is strange. You've always been her favorite."

"Did she say that?"

"Many times."

"I hope she's all right. Skylar tells me she isn't talking to anyone."

"Skylar. I heard that their marriage ended in a real donnybrook. They must have made up."

"She still hated him last time we talked. She told me that after the divorce she only put up with him so she could see her sister. She hated the way he kept Janice in debt."

"And now?"

"Now that Janice is dead, I can't understand why she lets him screen her calls."

"Is he with her all the time?"

"Yes. It's like they never got divorced."

I declined a cup of Jasmine's herbal tea and hurried on to the only other person in town I dared interview - Howard Running Horse. He was the head of the Indian Gaming Commission and ran the local casino.

I had known Howard since high school. I trusted him. I thought he could give me some information on the gambling syndicate.

The casino was in a handsome parlor on Chance Street. There was a small restaurant, pool hall and bar in the building. Howard had an office on the second floor.

After a half hour of reminiscing, I asked about the control of gambling in Camptown.

"It's all well run by the white guys. They've pressured me several times to give them a piece of the action, but I won't let them in. My partner, Jim Littlebear, disappeared a week ago. He was murdered gang style. I suspect that was the commission's way of telling me that I'd better play ball.

Now that you mention the possibility of Janice's murder, I remember that Jim spent some time talking to Skylar in the bar two weeks back. Skylar was real talkative when he was drunk. Maybe Jim knew too much about her murder.

Jim was found dead just yesterday. A friend told me that he saw someone in a red corvette dump him on a railroad siding and drive off. I don't know anyone that drives a red corvette.

"I've beefed up security at the Casino and have two body guards to look after me constantly. They are some of the roughest Indians I know. I pay them well just to keep them from being bought off."

I asked about Skylar. Howard knew Skylar was in deep debt to the gambling people. He was in debt to the

Casino as well, but all that came to an end shortly after Janice's death. His debts were paid in full.

I told Howard how I felt about the syndicate. He shook his head.

"If I were you, Matt, I'd be real careful asking any questions that might imply that your friend's sister was killed by any gambling syndicate."

As I drove back to my motel, I saw that I was being followed. Did Howard put someone on my tail?

I pulled up into the parking lot and noticed that my shadow followed in behind me. I didn't want any trouble. Maybe someone from the gambling syndicate had been following me all along.

I slipped from behind the wheel quickly and dashed for the motel lobby. Just as I reached the door a rough hand grasped my shoulder and turned me around. I was looking into the face of a tall husky Indian security officer.

"Howard asked me to keep you under my eye and I aim to go in with you." I saw no reason to argue. He did have a kindly smile.

There were two men waiting in my room. My shadow glided down the hall as if he had not been with me. Neither of my visitors noticed him.

They introduced themselves as Mike and Ed. Mike explained that they were working for Sam Strunk, the District Attorney. Mike was the spokesman. The other man never said a word. "You been asking around town about Janice Thomas's death. The DA wants you to button your lip and go back where you came from."

"I came from Rocky Creek. Is that what you mean?"

"Don't get funny." Mike reached into his coat and drew out a snub nosed revolver. "You see this? It will take away all your troubles."

Sweat popped out in all my pores. I had no idea that Sam Strunk could be so intense about a lone reporter from Plympton, Massachusetts.

"Perhaps the District Attorney would be kind enough to give me some additional pointers in his office tomorrow."

The man put up his gun. "I'll ask." He took a cell phone from his pocket and pushed a button.

"This is Mike – the pigeon wants to talk to you." There was a short pause. "Okay, I'll bring him over now." He folded the phone.

"Come on, let's go!"

I had no choice. As we left my room, I noticed a burly man taking a drink at the water cooler in the lobby. He winked as I passed him.

"You mean to tell me you're a reporter?" the District Attorney asked.

"Yes, with the *Plympton Paddock*. It's a rag with an exclusive clientele interested in horse breeding and racing."

"And you're also a friend of the Jelesco sisters."

"Only Janet."

"Am I to understand that you suspect that attorney Janice Thomas was murdered?"

"Yes. I think there is a strong possibility."

"Why?"

"I'm only a journalist but I smell a story here. Her body was cremated immediately, her daughter was not informed and members of the family as well as good friends are being kept from talking to Janet."

"Did you talk to members of the family?"

"I visited Jasmine. She wasn't disturbed by my visit. She has not been able to talk with Janet either and is worried about her."

The District Attorney turned to the two detectives that brought me in. "Leave us alone."

When the two tough guys had left, the District Attorney asked me to sit down. "So, who do you suspect killed my assistant?"

"Maybe Skylar, maybe the syndicate…"

"Careful when you say that word. You don't know that there is such a thing, and then if there is, that I'm not part of it"

"So what do I say – Skylar's gambling friends?"

"Okay – so how was it done?"

"You don't believe me, do you?"

"It doesn't matter, Janice had many enemies. If she was murdered, I'd have a lot of people to question. I'm just going after those friends you mention. If I get them, I'll get the whole bunch."

"So you are suspicious too?"

"Let's just say I'm a dedicated public servant."

"You mentioned enemies Janice had. Who are those people? I can only think of Skylar and his gambling friends."

"Nobody liked her. That's all I'm going to say. She even made me mad."

"You didn't like her?"

"Yeah, what's it to you? She was running against me in this year's election. She was a crackerjack attorney and I had a good chance to lose. I told her not to campaign on my time, but she had her own ideas of etiquette. She rubbed everyone the wrong way."

"I see. Can I stay in town long enough to finish my story?"

"Yeah. Just stay away from the Jalescos and the Thomases. Oh, and it wouldn't hurt to stay away from my boys either."

"That just leaves the syndicate – I mean Skylar's friends."

"You get the picture. Send Ed and Mike in as you go out. I need to fill them in on your stay."

Outside, I ran into the Indian officer. "Can you take me to the boss of the gambling commission?"

"I can take you there, but I won't go in with you. You're on your own in that place. I'll wait to see if you come out in one piece. If I don't see you again, I'll tell Howard that you couldn't be helped."

Buck – that was his name - took me to a roadhouse next to the track on the highway. The track was built on the only flat place around. It was built over a dry stream bed that had been leveled out. The roadhouse was dreary on the outside but appointed like a palace inside.

A very polite bouncer met me at the door, frisked me gently and knocked on the door of the office. There was a muffled answer from the other side that sounded like "Yes," and I was ushered in.

"Matt, how nice to see you."

I was surprised to see Benny Bernardo. He arose and extended his hand as I entered his office. I hadn't seen Benny in 20 years. He was the shortest guy in our high school class. I became his friend because he didn't seem to have anyone who liked him. My buddies liked him and found him to be a delightful fellow, but he was often the butt of all our jokes.

"Benny, I thought you were going to take over your father's bakery."

"Oh, Dad lost everything the year after we graduated. I've been with the horses ever sense."

"You seem to have done well."

"It's okay. We do better than pop did with Bernardo's Bakery. Did you know there are eight more Bernardos living in town, attributed to my wife and me?"

"That sounds great, Benny."

"My youngest has a real talent for painting. He sends somebody in New York three of his landscapes every month and there is a demand for more."

"What's his name, Benny? I'll look for his work when I'm back there next month."

"He goes by Vini, but he doesn't sign his name. You know how these young guys are. They just want to be anonymous. They think it's noble."

"I see." I didn't, but I let it go.

"Say, except for Howard, you are the only other member of our high school gang that's anywhere around. Ted, Frank and George got it in Vietnam and Jim Littlebear was murdered right here in town this month."

"So Jim was Howard's partner."

"Yeah, how'd you know?"

"Howard told me his partner was murdered."

"You saw him? I guess he thinks I did it. I couldn't wipe out an old friend like that."

"I guess not. What about Janice Thomas, Benny?"

"Oh, that. Well, Janice was no friend. She put two of my men behind bars, but they deserved it. I didn't do that either, Matt."

"Did Skylar kill her?"

"I don't think so. Everyone says it was an accident."

"Do you know different, Benny?"

"I've heard some things."

"Like what?"

"Well, Skylar owed me a lot of money. He liked the horses."

"So did he do it so he could get his hands on Janice's inheritance?"

"Inheritance? She had no inheritance. She just had a meager trust fund."

"No inheritance! So what happened to the Jalesco's fortune?"

"He's still got it."

"Who?"

"The old man? He's still alive?"

"Jalesco?"

"Yeah, Jalesco. He's the one who made it and he's hanging on pretty well."

"I never knew about him. What's he like?"

"You didn't know? He came here with an idea. It was all about horses. He came from Kentucky with a few breeders. He's the reason I have a job. Without him there wouldn't be any horse racing in Camptown. I thought you knew."

"Janet never mentioned him. She and her sister lived with their mother. I thought he died years before. They always seemed to have lots of money. I thought their mother owned the whole shebang."

"Oh, no. Ruben Jalesco had it all. He took care of his family, but he kept the rest to himself."

"So, Janice only had the trust fund? How did Skylar pay off all his debts then?"

"You heard about that! Yeah, he paid me and Howard too. He had a $250,000 policy on Janice. Lucky too, I was ready to foreclose on that fancy horse he has."

"Policy – I never thought of that. You know the company?"

"Something like Republic or New Republic. I remember the agent was real fussy. Even came here several times asking questions."

"Did he suspect murder?"

"Yeah, at first, but he didn't get anywhere with the Coroner or the District Attorney. Frankly, I think he just gave up.

"Janice's daughter was really upset that she got nothing. She's been here a month and has a big problem with Skylar."

"She thought she should have been on the policy? I don't see why. She and her mother haven't spoken for several years. That girl is one angry bambino. Maybe she murdered her mother?"

"No, I think it was an accident. Laura wasn't in town. She didn't even know about it until a week after the cremation."

After that, Benny and I settled into a discussion about old times. He had been real helpful. I wanted to believe that he had nothing to do with the death of Janice Thomas, but it had certainly worked in his favor.

I said goodbye to Benny, promising to talk to him later and went back to the motel. I reviewed my facts, called my editor and got a nice sleep.

Next day I thought I would visit Janice's daughter. Laura Thomas, it turns out, was staying at the Starting Gate too. Since she hated Skylar I saw no harm in visiting her.

She was nearly 18 years younger than I, but much more attractive than her mother. She greeted me with a smile. When I explained what I was doing, she became very friendly. We had lunch together and she pumped me for everything I knew.

The only thing I learned from her was that her grandfather, Ruben Jalesco, didn't like Janice or Janet. In her opinion he might be a prime suspect. I thought Skylar had a better motive.

I determined to see Ruben, even if his name was Jalesco. If he hated Janice maybe he hated Skylar also.

He lived in a villa up a torturous mountain road with his second wife and a multitude of children and grandchildren.

A guard stopped me at the gate; he was neither friendly nor gentle. He frisked me carefully and insultingly.

"What do you want here, Señor?"

"I came to see Ruben Jalesco."

"You won't see him. He doesn't see anyone."

"Tell him I think his daughter Janice was murdered."

The guard went into a little house by the gate, talked to someone on a phone, and returned.

As he approached my car, the gate opened abruptly. "Take the second left and drive up the hill. You can't miss his mansion. Good luck."

I didn't know quite how to take his "good luck", but I thought I might need it. He was right about the villa. I couldn't miss the mansion. It was tremendous. Hearst Castle had nothing on it. I drove right in the driveway and parked behind a red Corvette. "Your keys, Sir." A guard with a machine gun crossed my path and stopped beside my door.

I gave him my keys and he pointed to a door in the wall to my right. "Go in there!"

I followed his instructions and found myself in a dark passageway. At the end, I came to another door through which I heard strains of a Bach fugue. I tried the door. The knob didn't turn but a buzzing sound accompanied the inward swinging of the door. Another guard led me through a large well decorated room to an adjacent and smaller room - equally well appointed.

A man sat at a pipe organ. This could not be Ruben Jalesco. Then my eyes focused on a small shriveled old man seated near the organ smoking a cigar. He did not rise.

"Mr. Beckwith, please sit." I sat. He did not speak for several minutes, but seemed to be listening to the music. When the organist finished, Ruben waved his hand.

"Thank you Julian. That will be enough for now."

I reached my hand to Mr. Jalesco. He ignored it. "Mr. Beckwith, I read your column with interest when I get your paper. You are a very gifted writer. Would you tell me why you think my daughter was murdered?"

"I'm embarrassed to say that I thought it was for the Jalesco fortune. Nevertheless I still think money was the motive."

"Why is that?" Ruben took a long drag on his cigar.

"Because your son-in-law was so deeply in debt and because he won't allow anyone to talk to her sister."

"Janet hasn't talked to anyone?"

"No, not even with Jasmine."

"That is strange. You haven't been able to talk to Janet?"

"No and she and I have been good friends for many years."

"I see. I'd say you have a very big problem, Mr. Beckwith. What do you think I can do for you?"

"Does Janet stand to inherit any of your fortune?"

"She has a moderate trust fund. I think I've been generous to both girls considering that their mother poisoned them against me."

What about Laura? Will you leave anything to her?"

"I don't plan on dying soon, but there is a special allowance for her. Why do you ask?"

"Well, she's a pretty girl and clever too." I begged. "If she had a fair dowry, a guy like me might consider taking up with her."

"Oh, Mr. Beckwith, you aren't serious."

"No, not really. I just wanted to see how deep your dislike for Laura ran."

"Tell me, Mr. Beckwith. What's your real reason for coming here?"

"I was fascinated to know that you are still alive. I found out from my friend Benny that you are the reason for the success of this whole town. I didn't know that when I was a young man. I dated Janet. She never let on that she had a living father."

"Yeah, I guess she didn't. You're right about the town. It was nothing when I came here. It will be nothing when I check out. No one here has any imagination. I had hopes for Benny. I taught him all I know, but he's never been very creative. I had hopes for my second family, but they're content to be a rich man's kids.

"Now Janice and Janet, they were different, but they hated me and I reciprocated.

"Janice was a good prosecutor. She put several of her half-brothers in jail. Had she lived, she might have won the election.

"Most people don't know what a vixen she was. If somebody murdered her, they did me a favor. I won't have to watch my back so closely.

"I don't think you have a case for murder. That dumb fool Skylar milked her for all he could get. If he killed her, it was an accident.

"He needed her money and protection. He depended on the golden eggs she laid. I think that Janet helped him too because Janice couldn't handle his debts alone. I think he accidentally killed the Golden Goose so to speak."

The old man blew an acrid ring of smoke around my head and I knew the interview was over.

"Say hello to your editor for me. I've known Tom for a long time. He used to bet the horses here."

I went back to my motel. Laura was in the office when I asked for my messages.

"Are you checking out?" I asked.

"Not when I have all the goods on Skylar."

"What goods?"

She peered at me for a minute as if she were deciding whether to trust me or not.

"Come on a little drive with me and I'll show you."

"Okay." Why not, I thought.

I recognized the road we followed. It was the same one I traveled years before on my way to high school. It took the bus just 10 minutes to make it from Camptown to Rocky Creek, but Laura made it in 5 minutes and the road wasn't any better.

She didn't stop in Rocky Creek though. We drove through the little berg town of Castleton and up a dirt and gravel lane to Rocky Point.

"Just what do you hope to show me up here, Laura?"

"You'll see soon enough." She was confident as the dust roiled up around us and the rocks hit the bottom of the car. It was her car though, and I didn't try to slow her down.

We parked in the lot below the point. I had made this trip many times on a bicycle. It seemed a much shorter ride in the car.

She led me to some sharp rocks along the shore just below the cliff.

"This," she said with conviction, pointing up to the cliff above "is the place where my mother died from a fall, not a boating accident."

I looked up to the cliff. It was straight up. "A fall from up there would certainly have the same effect as being pulled into some rocks on the Lakeshore, Laura, but what brought you to this spot?"

"A man came to me in town today. He said he knew how my mother died and it wasn't in any boating accident. He was hunting out here the day she was killed. He was over in that draw when a man and two women drove up.

"They climbed up to the point. He saw them arguing about something and then the next thing he knew, mother came flying off the point and hit this rock. The man looked down from the point and smiled and then the woman got on a cell phone. A man came in a red corvette and helped with the body."

"Your witness probably told you that to get his name in the paper, Laura. Why would Skylar bring your mother way out here and kill her. It could just as well have happened anywhere. I read the coroner's report. Your mother was wearing a bathing suit. It was still wet. Her hair was wet. They left the boat and all at the cove along with the trailer. Why would they go to all that trouble?"

"I don't know, but I checked it out. There was no one at the lake because it was so cold that day. They'd have to be crazy to go waterskiing."

[43]

"Have you been up to the top, Laura?"

"No, I didn't expect to find anything there."

"You stay here. I'll go look."

I didn't know what to expect on the top. I was going to look for scuffle marks or a sign of a struggle that would confirm Laura's story.

Why would Janet be part of her sister's death? She loved her.

At the top were weeds and loose rocks. Even if I found something, it wouldn't necessarily prove that Skylar, or Janice or Janet were there. Young couples came here often. Sometimes they left items of clothing, jewelry even purses just to prove they'd been there.

The cliff was pretty clean. The wind was blowing and I tried to look through my fingers so as not to get dust in my eyes. As I started down, something red caught my eye. I retraced my steps, but saw nothing. Then, there it was – a red purse – just a small thing with cosmetics.

I took it down to Laura. There was nothing to identify it. It could've been anyone's.

Laura insisted that it was her mother's. I disagreed. I did stop to scrape some of the dark stains off the rock. It was like soft tar and I got a good sample.

Laura demanded that we drive over to the police lab in nearby Conway. An officer took the smear, agreed that it might be blood and promised to test it.

On a hunch, we took the purse to Aunt Jasmine. She spilled its contents out on her dining room table and sorted out the items with her fingers.

"They might be Janice's. The colors are right for both she and Janet." She said.

Women, I've learned, are very particular about colors. The lipstick and eye shadow colors that would match Janice's and Janet's hair and skin tones would be the same.

[44]

"Wait," Jasmine screamed as she came upon a tiny locket. "It's hers!"

"How do you know?"

"I gave it to her three years ago."

"You gave it to Janice?"

Jasmine looked at me in wonder. It took her a little while to get her composure.

"Not Janice – Janet. I gave it to her on her birthday."

I looked at Laura. She smiled - not a happy smile, but a smile of triumph. "They were there. I'm going to get that gigolo."

"Don't be hasty, Laura. They could have an explanation. Give me a chance to put it all together."

Jasmine was alarmed. "What are you saying? Is my Janet in trouble?"

I shared her alarm. Either Janet was being held hostage or she was in big trouble.

Laura agreed to give me time to see the results of the blood test. I planned to use that time to sift through the rest of my facts.

It seemed possible that no one else was immediately involved in the death. I couldn't believe that Benny encouraged it, but the man with the red corvette might have engineered the whole thing? Who has a red corvette?

Laura went to her room and I went to mine. What if the man and the woman on the cliff were Janet and Skylar? What if the man in the red corvette was really an accomplice? In any case, why would Janet be covering for the killer?

Just as I was telling myself that it had to be Janet and Skylar there was a knock at the door.

A little man stood there. "I am John Devereau from the new Pacific Life Insurance Company."

I resented his interruption but invited him in. "What can I do for you, Mr. Devereau?"

"May we sit down, Mr. Beckwith?" Everyone knew my name, even this little Frenchman.

"Of course." I was puzzled. What did he want with me?

"I understand you are interested in the death of Janice Thomas."

"Yes."

"Mr. Beckwith, would you mind sharing what you learned so far?"

Yes, provided you will share a few things with me."

He agreed and I told all except the business at Rocky Point. The only thing I learned from him was that Skylar had purchased a policy on Janice just five months ago. The policy had an accidental death clause and paid double indemnity. Even after the gambling debts Skylar would end up with nearly $500,000.

"There is one other thing, Mr. Beckwith. I've learned from another company that there was a policy for $200,000 more on Janice Thomas."

"So, Skylar stands to be a very rich man."

I did not like the way this was shaping up. Even Janet had a good motive in this mess.

Mr. Devereau straightened up in his chair. "Not Skylar, Mr. Beckwith, Samuel Strunk had the policy on Janice. You know, the District Attorney."

"The District Attorney? Did they pay it?"

"Yes. It was double indemnity too."

No wonder the District Attorney was so smug, I thought. What an opportunist!

I was tempted to tell the bit about Rocky Point, but now I had another person with a strong motive – one who might have manipulated Skylar and who had two strongmen with bad reputations.

He had hinted that he might be involved in the syndicate if there was one. His efforts to clean up the town were probably a cover-up.

Maybe Benny was in it too. I'd have to be real careful with whom I shared my "evidence".

It took three days for the blood work to come through. It didn't match Janice's blood type. Both Laura and I were disappointed. It was human blood but different than Janice's type recorded at the hospital.

Something about it bothered me. I compared it with the coroner's report. My copy showed an exact match for Janet. I did not tell Laura.

An awful sickness settled in my stomach. What if the lady cremated was not Janice Thomas? What if it was Janet Thomas? That might explain why no one could talk to Janet. Perhaps the lady taking her place was her twin sister.

I decided to test my theory. If Janet were dead, she would not be painting. I called her agent in New York. He was still receiving an average of three paintings per month. Funny, that was the same number that Vini was sending to New York each month.

In the morning I drove over to Janet's place. I just hoped that the District Attorney or his goons were not waiting for me. I sat in the woods in the front of the house for an hour. I thought no one could see me. I was determined to talk to "Janet" alone. Finally, Skylar left.

I rang the bell. Janet answered. I was sure it was Janet. She offered me a drink. She was cordial – even friendly. "Come in, Matt."

I stepped into the parlor. She gave me a warm embrace. This had to be Janet. She pulled away. "You came just in time, Matt. I want you to see what I'm working on." We went into a studio. Paintings lined the south wall.

The room was built out from the main house so that there were three walls of glass. A stream of soft northern light was focused on an easel in the middle of the room. There was fresh oil paint arranged on a pallet at a small table nearby. Fresh oil paint appeared to be on the canvas.

A landscape was taking shape on the unfinished picture. It was convincing.

I decided to play my trump card anyway. "Janet, in the past few days I've reminisced on our high school years. "Do you remember the goose you painted in our class?"

"I do. I think I still have it. Wait a minute." She left the room.

While she was gone, I touched the painting on the easel. Only linseed oil came off on my finger. It was not freshly painted, but was made to look so.

"Janet" returned with a 9 x 12 panel. "Is this it?"

"Yes. I remember how it looked when I first saw it. Do you recall what you said?"

"No. I don't know. Why don't you tell me?"

I looked at her a long time. "You said you were a goose - the Golden Goose in the picture."

"Why would I say a thing like that? The goose is white."

"I guess you thought you'd be a successful artist and everyone would expect you to lay golden eggs." I knew better. It wasn't Janet I was talking to. It was Janice. When Janet first painted the goose it was gold colored. She had told me that it was just the under coat.

I couldn't look at Janice. She looked so innocent. I gazed across the room.

"You know don't you?" she ventured.

"Yes."

"Was it something I said?"

"No. It was something you didn't say – something only your sister and I knew."

"Oh, Matt. What can I do? Skylar made me do it."

"What, murder your sister?"

"Oh, no. It was an accident, she…"

"Fell off the cliff?"

"How did you know? It was awful. Janet was drunk. She had a hard time climbing up to the point. We had to help her.

"When we got there, she kept twirling around and shouting that it was so beautiful. She told us that she was going to paint a panoramic landscape.

"She begged Skylar to take a picture of her and me. She insisted that we stand on the edge of the cliff so Skylar could get a good view of the lake behind us.

"She was drinking from a flask Skylar had with him. He shouted to warn us that we were too close to the edge. He came over to us to get his flask. Just as he reached out to get the flask, she lost her balance, spun around and dove over the precipice."

"She fell. That's some story, Janice."

"Don't you believe me, Matt? I've had no one to talk to – only Skylar. He had to have the insurance. It's all out of control. Strunk came in on it too. Oh, it was awful. They made me put Janet in my swimsuit. I kept saying this was not happening. Afterward they took the boat and skis down to the lake."

"The lake! Why would they do that?"

"To make it convincing perhaps. Oh, I don't know."

"Yes you do, Janice. Skylar pushed her off and you're covering up."

"No, he didn't. See, you think it was murder because we were on the cliff."

"Then she really did fall?"

"She did! She did! Skylar didn't push her. It's just that it looked bad – the three of us up on the cliff and the fall."

Just then, Skylar came in with Strunk and his two goons. "I brought your boss, Janice. He'll know what to do with Beckwith."

Outside the studio window I could see Skylar's car as well as the District Attorney's. Sam Strunk's car was a red corvette. Then there were two others cars. Laura was here. Heaven help the poor girl. Strunk and his tough guys would make short work of us. Still another car pulled up. It was Benny and his boys.

Where were they all coming from? Strunk didn't say a word at first – just came up and put the cuffs on me. If this was an arrest for something, he didn't read me my rights.

"I told you to stay away from the Thomases. Now we're going to have to plant you in the lake."

"You don't have to do that, Sam." Janice begged. "Let's just give it up. I've been through hell. Can't we just end it?"

"Not unless you want to end it with Matt."

There was a moment of nervous silence. Janice looked at Skylar as though wondering if he'd go along with the District Attorney. I could see that Skylar was weighing his chances.

"I'm with you, Sam." He said.

Janice shook her head. It was enough. She was not in accord with her boss on the killing.

"Okay, if that's the way you want it." Sam pointed to Janice and I. "Take these two out back and shoot them!"

Mike pulled out his snub nosed revolver. "Okay, boss."

Was Benny in on this? I thought. Where was Benny? For that matter, where was Laura?

As Mike and Ed escorted us out the front door, I caught sight of Benny's boys on either side. Sam's two tough guys didn't have a chance. Each got a hard knock on the head.

The District Attorney ducked back inside – a pistol in his hand. He headed through the kitchen to the back door.

There were a couple of shots and he staggered out of the kitchen and fell in the middle of the studio. Laura was behind him – a smoking pistol clutched in her hand.

Then, Benny came in. He smiled and I knew we were safe. "Thanks, Benny," I said. "Can you get these handcuffs off me? I've got a story to write.

Incidentally, you might want to know that Strunk survived and is doing time for the murder of Jim Littlebear. Janice dumped Skylar. She's the new District Attorney for Camptown. The citizens there are very forgiving and I got a nice fat bonus for my story. Incidentally, there is no syndicate in Camptown – there never was.

Geldergob and the Getsnips

A naughty person, a wicked man, walketh with a froward mouth. He winketh with his eyes, he speaketh with his feet, he teacheth with his fingers; Frowardness is in his heart, he deviseth mischief continually; he soweth discord. Therefore shall his calamity come suddenly; suddenly shall he be broken without remedy. (Old Testament / Proverbs 6:12 - 15)

Geldergob settled back and finished up his getsnips. He greatly cherished that dish. For the last few years he had relished getsnips so much that if they had been a fattening food, he would surely have died of "blubber-rot". Geldergob gave a sigh; getsnips were devilishly delicious; they were tasty to the point of addiction. The only thing that stopped him from continuing his most refreshing past time was that all the getsnips were gone; his plate was empty.

Somehow Geldergob never brought home enough of them, even though they could be ordered by the truckload. Till recently getsnips were rather scarce and very expensive. Now they were so cheap that a poor man could buy a year's supply with one month's wages.

The unusual plant from which the coveted fruit was gleaned had originated in the dense tropical jungle. It was said that primitive natives had carefully nurtured it into being. A Dr. Seemore J. Knowalot had won the Hick's title of the year for having discovered that getsnips were actually a hybrid breadfruit whose existence was owed to the mystical rituals and superstitions of this backward people.

According to Dr. Knowalot, getsnips were the native's source for a potion supposedly capable of destroying life. But if getsnips were intended to kill they were certainly a failure.

Undoubtedly, the more the primitive botanist crossed the plant the more frustrated he became, for everyone knew that getsnips were entirely safe to eat. In fact, now that they were completely marketable, getsnips were fast making it possible for even the hungriest wretch to sustain life and enjoying the delicacy of kings.

As Geldergob sat picking his teeth in the most aristocratic manner, his wife came bringing in the evening newspaper.

"Dear," she said, the way wives do when they are trying to cause their husbands to be concerned. "The market for getsnips is on the verge of disaster. The President reports that getsnip pickers earn so little now for their labor that they have planted trees in their own yards and refuse to report for work.

"Now, Sweetie," Geldergob wheezed, like husbands do who are sure their wives know nothing about everything. "I think that is perfectly wonderful! Everyone should have his own getsnip tree." And that was the day that Geldergob bought his first getsnip plant.

No one had a getsnip tree in Geldergob's neighborhood but all were anxious to pay him for the chance to pick getsnips for breakfast, lunch and dinner; and Geldergob obliged them by putting in several more getsnip trees around the house. The income was meager and it wasn't very long 'til everyone did have his own tree and neighbors became comfortable strangers once more.

Then one afternoon as Geldergob was enjoying his getsnips, one of these comfortable strangers suddenly became an irritable neighbor.

"It seems," he said, "that a horrible blight is absorbing all of the getsnip trees in central Toolulu and there is real danger that it will soon spread to all areas of the known world. People who own getsnip trees are asked to take every precaution to save them, as other foodstuffs are at a low in production, and some had actually gone out of fashion."

That was the year that Geldergob built the glass house and sanitary block building around his most productive getsnip tree.

For a while the price of getsnips soared quite high and then, with the discovery of anti-getsnip blight compound, the whole world sat back and made a habit of eating getsnips three times a day.

It was said that science was even on the verge of the discovery of a getsnip preserver that would protect the plant from anything that might come upon it. Getsnips were now supreme, and economic difficulties were at a standstill. Everyone was too secure and satisfied to move. Of course an established social protocol made everything seem normal.

Late one evening when Geldergob was finishing the last getsnip of the day, a very ordinary thought crossed his mind. Whether it crossed north or south or east or west, it still spelled out the same thing:

"How rich and famous would he be if Geldergob had the only getsnip tree?"

For the first time in many years he was really interested in doing something besides eat getsnips. So before the thought escaped him, he set his once industrious mind to work. He went to the nearest drive-in library and ordered all the books he could on the subject of getsnip blight. He did this, of course, under an assumed name so that the National Foundation For The Protection and Preservation of Getsnips would not be able to detect him once he had begun his wild scheme.

Carefully he studied out the possibilities of killing off the world's supply of getsnip trees without showing his hand. He found that even though the anti-getsnip blight compound had been effective in curbing the destruction of getsnips, no getsnip preserver had ever been successful.

Finally Geldergob decided to begin his sinister plan. Making a trip to the source spot of getsnip blight, he found a small unhealthy blight surviving on what was left of a once great orchard of getsnip trees. He took the fungus home and day by day fed it until it was strong and healthy.

Under cover of a secret bacteria proof shelter, Geldergob strengthened the blight until it was a hundred times more powerful than it had ever been before. Then, on numerous "vacation" trips, he planted the deadly destroyer. The results were fantastic. The nation's vast supply was ravaged overnight. Everything was done to preserve the getsnip plants but everything failed. Getsnips became dear; every edible herb in existence sold for gold and then at a terrible sacrifice to the owner.

While famine crossed the land, Geldergob ate getsnips. With apparently no concern for the lives that were lost because of his evil plan, Geldergob ate getsnips. Then, seemingly responding to a sense of civic responsibility, Geldergob came to the aid of the people. As the demand for seedlings and fruit grew larger and larger he became a rich man. Though he would not be persuaded to release the patents themselves to the public, he used his own funds to build more preservatories like the first and stocked them for the public.

Geldergob preservatories were going up all over the place and, every town that had one, placed a statue of the "great inventor" on top.

However, aware of his great plan, Geldergob would not be flattered into complacency. One by one he smuggled his super fungus into these proud shrines. By intentionally polluting each preservatory, he convinced the nations that no preservatory was safe. While it was believed around the globe that it would only be a matter of days before the horrible blight had destroyed even the best preserved getsnips, Geldergob sat back and enjoyed another plateful.

Wars spread rapidly but died abruptly for lack of provisions. Before it was discovered that Geldergob had the only secure getsnips, everyone was too weak to confiscate his property. Billionaires lined up in front of his house each day and paid a thousand for a single plateful and the nation's greatest engineers and architects did hand labor for getsnip wages. By spring they had completed a summerhouse for Geldergob atop what once was the national gold reserve. Finally the cost of getsnips got so high that only Geldergob and his wife were left to feed upon the getsnip tree.

Then one morning when Geldergob's supply of getsnips was running low he went out to fetch some fresh ones. As he entered his preservatory, he noticed that it was covered with a spidery thatch. It had no apparent meaning for Geldergob as he went through the various stages of purification, and when he entered the final lock he was perfectly satisfied that his highly prized and dearly cherished getsnip tree was well preserved. But then as he entered the observatory room where he could look into the glass covered chamber, an eerie green glow seemed to shower down on his precious delight. There before his eyes the getsnip tree was absorbed to nothing.

Geldergob settled back and finished up his getsnips. He greatly cherished that dish. For the last few years he had relished getsnips so much that if they had been a fattening food, he would surely have died of "blubber-rot". Geldergob gave a sigh; getsnips were devilishly delicious; they were tasty to the point of addiction. The only thing that stopped him from continuing his most refreshing past time was that all the getsnips were gone; his plate was empty.

The Ghost of Petersham

Blessings are upon the head of the just: but violence covereth the mouth of the wicked. The memory of the just is blessed: but the name of the wicked shall rot.(Old Testament | Proverbs 10:6 - 7)

I shall never forget playing as a child on the hill of Mirabel. By then it was just a big grassy hill with a few old stones.

We used to recite a rhythm about Mirabel. "Never more shall sunlight glow on Mirabel's golden shrine." I didn't know where the verse came from and I doubt that any of us knew what it meant.

It was often cloudy on the hill, but just as often the sun brightened the old stones at the top that were supposed to represent Mirabel's shrine. True enough one of the stones did have what looked like a picture of Mirabel roughly sculptured into its surface. That was not much of a shrine to me even then.

On the East side, where the hill began to sloop out gently, were the remains of an old tower, or so it looked. All around it were stones sunk in the rich brown clay and grass grew up so as to almost hide the old ruins.

Some said the grounds were haunted during the day by a young man who was called Rufus. Others claimed an old man by the same name roamed the premises by night. None of us would go there at night, but we played that we were knights and ladies there on summer days.

At that time Petersham was a small village near the coast. I doubt anyone lives there now, but it was home in my younger years.

Some say that the village got its name from the Keep just below Mirabel's Shrine. We could imagine that some sort of castle lay there beneath the sod, but it was difficult to think that it was very big.

Not too far from Petersham was an old monastery. It was isolated from the village and everything else around. When I was older and doing research in the area, I visited the monastery and was privileged to examine some old manuscripts recorded by the monks.

I could not decipher the ancient text, but when I came across the name Mirabel, I asked one of the monks to translate for me. From the beautiful hand written script he read:

"The Grand Duke Rufus took the Keep,
Old Petersham by name
And no one called him king that day
Nor did they give him fame

The King and Queen were never found
Nor royal heir to claim
And all souls mourn their loss
As terror ends their reign.

So tortured, bled and taxed to death
The people made a plan
They took old Rufus to the tower
And killed the dreadful man.

Once dead, they mourned King Peter
And his fair wife, the queen
And their son, Rufus Miraba
Their graves were never seen.

Yet still we hear upon the hill
The tears of damsels crying
They mourn for good Queen Mirabel
And all her family dying.

Though no one knows

Their resting place
Nor how they met their God
They mourn for those
Who must be laid beneath the green, green sod.

O Mirabel, our Mirabel,
We've built our Queen a Shrine
We long for you, we cry for you
Oh, come and grace our glen.

And bring us back our worthy King
With Miraba your son
So light will grace our mound
O Mirabel, our Mirabel,
 Where else can you be found?

They mourn and mourn
From sun to sun
And beg for grace below
But never more shall sunlight glow
On Mirabel's golden shrine.

I wondered at the story that unfolded in those few verses. I pondered it long and well. I asked as many of the old timers that still lived in the area.

One day I had a strange visitor. He wore ragged clothes and seemed a homeless, but happy old codger.

I was sitting alone on my porch enjoying the sunset. I chanced to look around as though following the panorama of the strikingly colored sky and he was there. He stood there like a statue in a game of "Mother May I". He seemed to be waiting for someone to ask him a question before he would move.

"What!" I murmured as I turned.

"Your lordship will make a nice trip to the ruins this evening with me, will-ya?" His question was more of a statement.

"Why would I do that?" I asked.

"Why, to see Rufus." He answered as though I had been thinking of him all day long.

"I'm afraid I am not very much interested in the myth of Rufus."

"But it's not really a myth, my Lord." He approached 'til he could almost breathe in my nostrils.

"And what will Rufus do?"

"He'll tell you what you want to know about the boy and his parents."

At this point I became very interested. "Are you inviting me to accompany you?"

"That I am, sir. It's just a little walk from here."

"That I know from my youth."

"Oh, yes I remember you."

"I'll get a coat. Will you be warm enough on the hill."

"Indeed I will. Don't you worry for me, sir." And so our journey began - he, leading the way and I strolling cautiously behind.

I don't know what my expectations were up there on Mirabel's hill. Perhaps I hoped to learn something I never had the spine for when we were young. As we ventured up the winding path the withered old man mused half to himself and half to me.

"Old Rufus will be glad to see his old friends. That he will."

As we came to the brow of the hill, a chill wind began to blow across the grass. It was winter now and the cold bit into my bones. The grass was dry and crackled some in the breeze.

"We'll soon see the old ghost, sir."

The sun had set and the afterglow barely revealed the scattered stones as I remembered. One I'd forgotten stopped my foot and I searched for my balance like a drunken sailor.

The moon peaked over the crest and cast eerie shadows over the ruin. It was easy to imagine all sorts of strange spirits there among the stones. What took our breath though was not a ghost, but a very real figure that stepped suddenly from the remains of the tower. He wore a long coat and carried a gun.

"Stop right there, governor. I'll take your purse and any other valuables you might have on your person."

The codger laughed so hard I thought he had set me up, but when he caught his breath, he introduced me to Michael Collins, a local bandit who, I remembered hearing, always worked alone. Collins was polite but a little rough in his search to assure himself that I had nothing more than a few farthings.

"Why you're nothing but a student, son. What brings you up to the ruins at night?"

"I played here as a boy," I blustered as he prodded my body. "This gentleman promised to show me the ghost of old Rufus if I followed him tonight. I would never have done such a thing as a lad."

"I'll wager you wouldn't come again. Anyone in his right mind would never come up here at night unless he was an Englishman."

"Oh, I'm not an Englishman, Mr. Collins."

"I can see that, lad, and you're not much for money either. Would you have something back in town to help a poor man? I could use a few pounds right now."

"Like you said, sir, I'm just a poor student myself, but I hope to make a pound or two from the story I plan to write of this place."

"Do you think this old man can uncover the secrets that lie here when your own youthful curiosity never paid you a farthing?"

"I'm older now myself and such things as happened here are weightier these days."

"I see. Well, this man may know something of Mirabel, but I can tell you more about this place than a host of men can give you."

The robber's boast was tantalizing to my ears and I sat on the rocks there with him and the codger until morning listening as the history of Mirabel was unraveled across the centuries. This is his story:

"Peter and Rufus were brothers and young Rufus was named for his uncle. There was not much in this land then, but Peter was king. Since his people raided their neighbors and their neighbors raided in return, Peter was more like king of the bandits.

"Queen Mirabel was not a party to the craft of her people. She came of a good family of royal blood. Whatever she touched turned to goodness.

"It was not long until Peter became a princely gentleman. He swore off the evil of his realm and fostered the keeping of sheep and the making of cloth.

"His people began to prosper under his rule and the kingdom grew as their neighbors left off the wicked role and followed the example of Peter and Mirabel.

"Rufus was not so. He had no Mirabel to reform him. What Peter had, Rufus wanted, but he feared the people. He must devise a plan to dispose of Peter and Mirabel and their heir apparent quietly and without alarm."

"So how did he dispose of the three?"

"The exact way eluded him until one day he chanced to find his nephew playing knights in the dungeon. The boy was looking for someone to lock up in the cells.

"When his uncle came down, the youth asked him to be his prisoner. Rufus the elder willing entered into the game, but when he found himself caged up for a long period of time, he thought of a plan to rid himself of Peter and his family."

"And what was that?"

"Be patient. Now let's see where was I? Oh yes, when young Rufus returned, Uncle Rufus persuaded the young man to take his place. Once the boy was caged, Rufus the elder conveniently lost the key.

"He pretended annoyance and then despair so the story goes. He advised his brother of the problem. No one could find another key, so they brought blankets and food and nursed the boy, hoping that the cage could be breached in due time.

"The King and his Lady were beside themselves and much distracted that they could not be at his side to comfort him. They sent for a blacksmith, of course, but all that took time.

"In the meanwhile, they became so unhappy with the narrow passage that afforded them access to their son that they entered into an adjacent cell. This was the advantage that old Rufus was looking for.

"As though he had no sense or was just clumsy, he pushed the door shut on them and it locked. Now there was no key for this cell either and in despair the royal family pleaded with Uncle Rufus to bed and nourish them until the blacksmith arrived.

"Needless to say, he did nourish them, but the blacksmith never did arrive. Rufus now had the power to rule and no one to deny him the pleasure of his own wishes. In effect, he was now the King."

"How shrewd! Did anyone discover his deception?"

"Awe, there were many: the servants, his trusted knights, his friends. Each in his turn discovered the secret of the dungeon of Petersham and one by one they were tortured until they swore allegiance, or they died for their loyalty to King Peter."

[63]

"So how did the people come to know King Rufus' subterfuge?"

"Oh, the people were wily too, don't forget, like meself they were robbers and plunderers. They soon began to hear from men who had taken the oath, but had found themselves out of the reach of their king and able to talk.

"But that was not all. They also began to chafe under the rule of Rufus. His taxes were enormous and impossible. His demands for security drained the people of their young men and his desires for a companion frightened the mothers of the town.

"In the end they overcame his guards, took over the castle and threw Rufus from the tower. They hoped then to learn of their beloved king and his queen.

"They looked for their graves, some communication of their banishment, or imprisonment, but King Rufus had covered his sins well. He died with his secret. Only he had fed the good king and his family. Only he knew the way to the dungeon that he had covered with stone and made accessible through a hidden door.

"When the entrance was found it was too late. Good King Peter, his wife, Mirabel and their son, Rufus were all dead."

"What an amazing story! Where is this dungeon now? Can you show it to me?"

"Oh, no one knows today, my lad. It's beneath all this ruin someplace, but unless you dug up the whole of it, you'd never know."

For brevity's sake I have shortened the story somewhat, but for the most part this is the tale told by the robber of Petersham. As I've said, it was dawn when he finished. The old man had seemed to sleep, but as the sun rose over Mirabel's shrine, the old codger stood and smiled. "I know where the dungeon is."

"Don't listen to him, my boy. He's no wiser than I on the matter."

The old man said nothing, but picked up a rock and tossed it off into the grass. Instead of falling as we supposed in the grass with a plunk the rock fell down into some sort of crack in the earth. We could hear it ricochet of the walls of a well or some other underground cavern.

Mr. Collins looked long and hard at the place where the rock would have landed. He rose and I also. The three of us met where the grass parted and focused on a crack in the ground. I stooped and brushed the dirt aside. Beneath the dust was hard rock. I moved a few loose stones and there reaching up to me in what looked like an old air shaft was a bony hand – a small hand – that of a boy – perhaps the ghost of young Rufus.

The Magic Hat

The integrity of the upright shall guide them: but the perverseness of transgressors shall destroy them. Riches profit not in the day of wrath: but righteousness delivereth from death. (Old Testament / Proverbs 11:3 - 4)

Young Finkle leaned back in his swivel chair, admired himself in a pocket mirror and gave a sigh. What a handsome young fellow he was! A scant 30, just four years out of law school and already the "Finkle" of Greathouse, Throwbridge and Finkle. So far his future looked promising. As a bright young attorney in the business of patents and copyrights, there seemed to be endless opportunities open to him.

He had to laugh, though. Before him stood the dumbest assortment of time savers and automation ever devised by man. At first glance, anyone could tell that more than half of these pathetic gimmicks were worthless. The rest were about as marketable as second hand shoestrings. However, someday he would snag a real inventor. He was in no hurry. Money was the least of his worries.

"Mr. Finkle," Judy's voice chirped on the intercom. "There's a gentleman here to see you about an object we have that belongs to him. To hear him talk it's a marvelous piece of equipment."

Well, then, possibly today was the day. "Send him in, Judy; and . . . ah, Judy, pull his application and bring it in."

"He has no application on file, Mr. Finkle. I checked."

"No application?" Must be something recent, "Well, who is he?"

"He won't say – just demands to see you."

Today must be the day, "All right, let him in!"

No sooner had Finkle released the switch on the intercom than the door burst open and there stood a very handsome old gentleman in a rather eccentric looking suit.

"May I help you?" Finkle rose respectfully and offered his hand.

"You robbed me!" The old man ragged, refusing to take Finkle's hand.

"There must be a mistake, sir. My secretary suggested that you have an object worthy of a patent."

"No such thing! Where have you put my hat and the money? I do not intend to prosecute you. Just return my goods!"

Judy, who had followed the gentleman into Finkle's office, reflected the puzzlement in her boss's face. "If you would tell Mr. Finkle what you are missing, I'm sure he will help you. If he has anything at all of yours, he will certainly return it."

"What am I supposed to have taken?" Finkle groped for an understanding, "Is it something you left for a patent search?"

The old man hesitated as though disoriented, "Perhaps, I've missed my timing," he muttered, as though talking to himself; "however, I can't be too far off." Then to Finkle once more, "You apparently do not connect me with your escapade in my hat."

"A hat! You feel I have your hat? I have many fine hats. Is it any of these?" Finkle indicated a shelf beside his desk, hoping to placate his accuser.

"You know the one!" Roared the codger, raking the hats to the floor with his cane. He was next to Finkle now – talking loudly in his ear. "It is a hat exactly like this!" And he threw his hat on the desk.

"But I have no other hats!"

"You lie! You used it yourself."

"See here, I don't even wear a hat."

"You did! You used it to rob me. You took my money! You are a thief and a liar!" As he finished his accusations, the man turned on Finkle with his cane.

"You're out of line, you old coot. Calm down!" Finkle demanded as he dodged each thrust and swing.

Judy dashed out and returned shortly with two other men - the very respectable Greathouse and Throwbridge. Before very long the three of them had wrestled the strange not-so-gentle old man to the floor and hustled him off to jail, still venting a hail of wrathful pronouncements.

Finkle straightened his tie and set about picking up all the hats that lay on his office floor. Among them was the old man's hat that had fallen to the floor during the scuffle. It had a special style about it. As he was unbending, Finkle became aware that his secretary was still present.

"Are you all right?" She spoke just above a whisper.

Finkle dropped the hat on his desk and took a halting breath of air. The sparing bout with the cane had ruffled his composure. He staggered than sat down.

"Can I get you something?"

Finkle stared up at her helplessly.

"I mean you look like you could use a drink of water." His gaze drifted around the room. More silence. Concerned and frightened, the young secretary backed toward the door, her pretty painted lips still parted with her last useless suggestion.

Finally, just as she was about to turn, Finkle looked her full in the face and spoke. "Sit down, Miss Cassidy!"

"Yes, Mr. Finkle." she said, gliding into the chair next to the door.

"There is no reason for that old man's action."

"No, Mr. Finkle."

"He was obviously out of his mind – an eccentric inventor or just a plain everyday crazy. We haven't anything belonging to him – well, we have this hat, but he just now left it here."

"Don't let it bother you, Mr. Finkle. There's nothing we could have done to . . ."

"It's strange isn't it, Miss Cassidy?"

"Everything about that man was strange."

"No, I mean this hat especially," Finkle said poking the hat. "Have you ever seen one anything like it?"

"I suppose not."

Finkle turned it over. "It's just a hat, no wires, no knobs, no gages. It's rather good looking but . . . "

"He was just crazy, Mr. Finkle; may I go now?"

"Yes, of course, but before you go," Finkle rose and came around the desk, "take the hat, Miss Cassidy."

"Oh, I couldn't." Judy shrank into her chair."

"It won't hurt you." Miss Cassidy took the hat.

"There, now wouldn't you say it was a little heavy for what it seems to be?"

"Why yes, I believe it is." She handed it right back." May I go now? It's past break time and if you're all right . . .?"

"Oh, of course – and take your time. I suppose I should thank you for saving me from that nut." Finkle smiled down on Miss Cassidy and politely extended his hand as she rose from the chair."

"Thank you." There was an exchange of glances and then she was gone. It was as though Miss Cassidy could not decide which man was crazier.

Finkle settled down to reflect and examine the hat more closely. Perhaps he would even tear it apart to see why it was a little heavier than it should be.

It was round on the top – somewhat like a bowler hat – made out of felt and hard or perhaps firm – no, hard was the right expression. It did not give – perhaps it had a metal or plastic lining. Finkle shook it. He was looking more closely at its inner lining when Mr. Greathouse's voice boomed out at him from the intercom.

"Come in here, Finkle, we want to talk to you!"

Catapulted from a world of tiny fibers and specks of lint, Finkle hit the response button on his intercom so hard that the machine almost flew off his desk.

"Yes, Mr. Greathouse. I'll be right in."

The hat was forgotten. Finkle made his way around the desk through the outer office furniture and into the inner sanctum of the senior partners like a star half back carrying the ball over a field of assailants.

Mr. Greathouse and Mr. Throwbridge were standing side by side when he entered.

"Don't you ever knock?" Mr. Greathouse winced a little, trying not to disclose his surprise or the pleasure he felt at having extracted utter and swift obedience of his junior counselor.

"I – I thought you expected me – I . . ." gasped Finkle.

"You thought! You thought! Well, Mr. Finkle, see that you handle yourself with more decorum!"

"Yes, Mr. Finkle," Throwbridge added, "You could have put on your jacket too."

"I didn't realize . . ." Finkle panted.

"That is quite all right." Greathouse stated with condescension and they all sat.

"Your work here is at best mediocre, Finkle. If it were not for your marriage to my daughter I would have to ask you to leave. You know that you are just riding on my coat tails. You haven't earned a dollar for this firm in the whole year you have worked here."

"But I had no idea, your daughter, I thought that . . ."

"Oh, come, come now, my boy! You married my daughter just to get me to take you in. I had hoped that you might become as a son to me, but you are a blemish on this partnership."

"What can I do, sir? I . . ."

"You can start by explaining this scene in your office . . ." Throwbridge chimed in.

"Don't rush the boy, Throwbridge."

"The scene in my office?" The probability that Greathouse would lay the blame for the incident at his feet was a surprise to Finkle.

Greathouse turned to Throwbridge, "You see, Throwbridge," Greathouse injected, "he doesn't even know there was a scene. He probably doesn't know there is such a thing as money either."

"Well, I had not thought of it as a scene, but I know money."

"Shut up, my boy!" Boomed the head of the firm.

"You only make your position worse." The number two man echoed.

Greathouse and Throwbridge were a solid team. It was obvious that they had planned this whole effort.

"You see," Greathouse continued, "we think this old codger is some relative of yours – probably trying to take advantage of your position here."

"Yes, maybe even your father," Throwbridge mused.

"There is quite a resemblance." Greathouse rose and sat on the edge of his desk. Looking down at Finkle, he searched the young man's face. Finkle only blinked back. His face taut, his lips set. He was putty ready to be molded.

"Well, in any event, Finkle, the whole thing was shabby. What was this man's claim on you?"

"I don't know. He said I had stolen something – a hat I think – maybe some money – but . . ."

"You have no record?" It was a statement more than a question. "Probably something you forgot to write down, Finkle?"

[71]

"Oh, no sir!"

Throwbridge entered the interrogation at this point, stepping up beside the senior partner so that he also looked down on Finkle. "Then why would he single you out?"

"I don't know the man!" Finkle turned on Throwbridge, selecting the lesser of his two antagonists. "He just came in and started shouting – you saw how he was behaving – not at all sane."

"I suppose we'd better lay off, Throwbridge. The boy's probably right – just another crazy."

Throwbridge was resentful. Greathouse had turned him off again. He was steamed – ready to let Finkle have it and just when it was his turn to have a lick at the prey – Bingo. It was a typical put down which Greathouse had sucked him into time after time.

"Just a minute, Greathouse." Throwbridge was livid. "This boy may have done us irreparable damage. The case is not closed! This could cost us thousands of dollars."

"What do you mean? Throwbridge, old boy." Greathouse humored him along.

"Well," blurted Throwbridge, "he could have made us vulnerable to a law suit."

"How so?"

"We did take the old man by force."

"Yes, I see what you mean."

"I don't." Finkle joined in.

"What Throwbridge is saying, my boy is that even crazies have legal representatives and everything that happened here could receive an entirely differed orientation in a court of law. The fact that you do not know anything about the man could even work against us."

"We must be sure that none of this man's claims can be substantiated." Throwbridge was beginning to feel reassured.

"But how could they?" Finkle was baffled. "I have told you I did not take his money or his . . . "Finkle paused, then his eyes widened. "His hat!"

"His hat?" The two senior partners fixed their eyes on Finkle.

" Yes, it's in my office. He threw it on my desk during the argument."

"Oh, no!" Throwbridge was in pain. "We must get it back to him!"

"No!" Greathouse shot back. "It would be like a confession of guilt. Make a memo, then a receipt. You, Finkle will take him a copy of the receipt and find out if he is represented by counsel. Find out as much as you can – his address, his line of work, everything."

Throwbridge was embarrassed again. His partner was right of course. They should keep the hat but take every precaution. He cast in his mind for some shortcoming in Greathouse's plan - still playing the game.

"What if this bumpkin drops the ball?"

"We'll hire a private investigator, Throwbridge. You take care of that. He can report to you. Have him visit the man as well and keep a record of visitors so we might track them later if necessary."

The game was played out. Both men seemed satisfied with their performance. Neither had been shammed. Only Finkle had lost. After all, he was the junior partner. He was supposed to lose.

Finkle left the office quite disturbed that day. He felt like buying a dog so he would have something to kick. There was no percentage in kicking his wife verbally or beating her once he got home. All of that would get back to papa and he could ill afford to further discredit himself. Instead he chose to discuss the whole matter with Harriet and hope that he might borrow some idea from her that could be used against her father. He sensed rather than knew that children often can do more damage to parents than competitors.

"You really should see this man as soon as possible, Myron. What was his name?"

"Oh, of all the dumbness, I didn't get it."

"His name?"

"Right. He wouldn't give it at first and I didn't check to see if he had given it to the arresting officer."

"No matter. You can ask when you see him."

"How will I ever find him without a name?"

"Silly! Your name must be on the report."

"Oh. Do you think he will tell me his name? He didn't before and now we've put him in jail." Finkle was beginning to feel a slight remorse for having put the old man in jeopardy.

"Probably not, but you have to try. You must go before he gets loose on bail. He may be very hard to find later."

"You go, Harriet. He can't dislike you. Maybe you could just be a visitor and find out about him without his knowing."

"Well, I could, but are you sure that's a good thing to do? Father is expecting you to prove yourself in this matter I'm sure and . . . "

"But don't you see? They are even getting a private detective to do their job. Won't this show initiative?"

"I think they'll just believe you are afraid to go yourself."

"Go for me Harriet. I don't care what they think. You'll do well. I know you will."

The matter was settled. Harriet dressed and left Finkle to eat alone. Taking some cookies in a bag, she started out for the city jail.

The old man looked strikingly familiar as Harriet watched him enter the visitor's room. She had learned from the arrest record that his name was M. C. Finkle. Perhaps an uncle or cousin who Myron had forgotten.

"I'm Harriet."

"Yes, I know. How could I forget . . .?"

"Well, I certainly have. You look familiar, but . . ."

"Oh, that's all right . . ."

"Are you Myron's uncle or . . ."

"Certainly not!" He was shocked that she would assume such a thing.

"I'm sorry. You do look a little like Myron, but – ah . . . more mature and ah . . . distinguished."

"Thank you, but we are really not relatives!"

The man was positive in his manner. Apparently he had used his short time behind bars to advantage. He was not the rash abusive individual Myron had described.

"We can sit here" Harriet motioned to two vacant chairs. "I brought you some cookies. You do like cookies don't you?"

"Well, of course. Are they the cinnamon dainties? I mean are they by any chance cinnamon dainties?"

"How did you know?"

"The aroma of cinnamon, I guess." He took one from the bag and examined it with reserve but there was hunger in his eyes as though he would like to devour the whole bag and Harriet too. Harriet warmed. Her face flushed a little.

"You are a lovely woman, Harriet, and the cookies are most welcome."

"Your hat is safe." Harriet was glad of something formal to say. "My husband asked me to give you this receipt."

"Then, he did have my hat?" The man seemed not to grasp the fact that he had just left his hat during the arrest. Then, his eyes brightened as if a great secret had dawned in his mind. "I'm sorry, I see it all now. I am a

[75]

victim of time. I did miscalculate. The whole thing is my fault."

"You are speaking in riddles as far as I'm concerned, Mr. Finkle."

"Yes. That must be. Perhaps I will explain it to you later."

"I would like that. Will you be here long? I mean, will bail be posted?"

"I doubt it. Unless, perhaps you could find me a good attorney who could be patient with his fee."

"I'd be glad to – if I can. Maybe I could get my husband to drop the charges."

"That would be even better."

"Do you have family? Could I contact someone for you and let them know where you are?" Harriet was earnest in her offer.

"No. There is no one who knows me here. Will you come again? I may be here a while before . . . "

"Surely!" Harriet felt sorry for the old man. She wanted to visit him. It would probably help if she could get him to explain the riddle of the hat. She took his hand in hers and gave it a squeeze as they both rose. He turned away and left the room. Harriet guessed the cookies would shortly be gone. She must bake some more cinnamon dainties.

Myron Finkle was livid when she got home. "I looked all over for the cookies. I can smell them, Harriet. I've gone all through the house. Where did you hide them?"

"I took them to the old man!" She threw her gloves on the table.

"All of them!" Myron left her in the hall and walked into the living room to hide his disappointment.

"He needs them more than you do. Besides, can you think of a better way to loosen his tongue?" Harriet fluffed her hair as she followed Myron.

"I guess you're right. You always are. What did you find out?"

"His name is Finkle and his initials are M C. just like yours, but he says he's no relation."

"Maybe he's lying. Your father thought he looked like me."

"He does look like you, only more mature."

"You think I'm immature?"

"I didn't say that. He's simply like a grown up, more experienced copy of you."

"Copy! That's not very flattering. He's got wrinkles and gray hair. Did you get his address?"

"No. He says he has no one here to go to – no attorney, no money, nothing. You must drop the charges against him, Myron."

"Why? He attacked me; he may attack me again."

"Oh, I don't think so. He's a most charming and level headed individual."

"I see. Will you take him more cookies?" There was jealousy in his voice, but Harriet chose to ignore it.

"If you want me to." This put Myron on the spot. He guessed that another visit would be helpful to his career, but he couldn't be happy about the cookies. There was something else bothering him - his wife's interest in the old man. He did not dare put this into words. There was a part of Harriet's life he no longer shared. It was like that part of his mother's life that she shared with his father. He held his breath a little, doubled his fist and turned away.

"Oh, go ahead. Do whatever you think is necessary." Myron would resent his own license later, but there it was. It made him feel in control. Perhaps it freed him of childish thoughts and memories of long ago which he wanted to forget.

Reflecting on the matter the next day did not help. He was writing a memo to his father-in-law. The whole idea of sending Harriet was distasteful now. The clandestine nature of the escapade did not over shadow his cowardice. On paper the spark of friendship between Harriet and this rather good-looking old man was more apparent. How else could he explain to her father the enthusiasm with which she undertook the project or his continued reluctance to see the man?

He bitterly penned statements like: "Harriet seems to have a way with him. Harriet is far more successful than I could have been because he is obviously a very lonely man." He could not bring himself to say, "Because she is clever that way."

Then there was her request to drop the charges. He could not use the reasons: "because she thinks he is charming and harmless." Greathouse saw how "harmless" the old man was. The "charming" old man was a real threat – both legally and physically with emphasis on the physical. Finkle tore up the unfinished memo.

But Mr. Greathouse already knew that Harriet had taken Myron's place. Throwbridge's detective reported immediately.

"What do you mean sending my daughter after that old coot?" Greathouse shouted as he burst into Finkle's office. "You were supposed to go!"

"I – I did not think it wise." Finkle had never seen Greathouse this agitated. It was frightening, but the effect was worth the terror Finkle felt. If he could ruffle the distinguished Greathouse, maybe there was hope for him in this world.

"That geezer could be just toying with her," Greathouse continued. "Once he gets us to drop the charges, he could sue. Did she get any information from him? The detective said she got nothing – nothing! She got no address, no attorney, no relatives, and no nothing!" Finkle smiled at Mr. Greathouse's use of the word "got". He never used that word. It was amusing to see him so strung-out. On the other hand the idea that the elder Finkle

[78]

might be toying with Myron's wife set young Finkle off. He was not a fool. He stood up.

"There's no harm in taking an old man some cookies. A second batch will prove that I am right. She'll obtain all the information we want!" Finkle was proud inside. The roar of his own voice had driven the doubts he felt out of his mind. For once he had faced the senior counselor with defiance.

"Well, we will not drop charges!" Greathouse spat as he turned to leave.

"I wouldn't think of it!" Finkle shouted after him. His mind was fixed on that point. Another reason was just frosting on the cake.

Harriet combed her hair and refreshed her lipstick in the mirror of her car before she entered the city jail. Her step resembled a horse's gallop on her way to the barn.

"M. C. Finkle," she signaled as the clerk came to the desk.

"I'll arrange to have him come to the visitor's room. Would you please sign in?"

Harriet quickly wrote her name and vital statistics on the ledger and proceeded down the hall. In the visitor's room she paced up and down until Mr. Finkle appeared.

"How nice of you to come again so soon, my dear."

"I – I came because you said you might explain."

"I see." The old man was hesitant. "Did you want to know for you or for Myron?"

"You said that the scene that you caused was all your fault. I would like to know how that is possible. You seem so gentle that I hardly believe the things that I have heard."

"I am very sorry for my outburst, Harriet. I did act in a very disturbing way."

"My husband must have provoked you. He is very short tempered and can often behave unreasonably. Sometimes I wish I had never married him." There was a tear in Harriet's eye.

"There, there my dear." They were both very near and as Harriet began to cry, the old man reached out to comfort her. Harriet's reaction was automatic. She put her head on his shoulder and sobbed.

The senior Finkle pushed her away gently and, taking a handkerchief from his pocket, offered it to her. She dabbed her eyes dry.

"Thank you. I'm so sorry."

"That's all right. I understand perfectly. I have had a lot of time to think about Myron while I have been here in the jail. I have also had time to think of my life as I grew older than Myron. I can see that I made a lot of bad decisions. I am sorry. I think that I have mellowed some as I have matured. You will see. Myron will change and you mustn't blame him for my actions."

"But he has been so hard on me. He thinks that I want to live just like my parents, but I don't need that. He and my father don't get along and so he takes it out on me. When he's home, he eats, he watches TV and he sleeps. We almost never go anywhere together – even for a walk."

"Well, my dear, when he gets to be as old as I, he will have had much more experience and become a very gentle person. He will realize how wonderful you are and won't be able to do without you. You can count on it."

"That's very hard for me to believe. Look at my father. He's older and he is anything but gentle. Even though Myron hates my dad he thinks his success depends on his becoming just like him. He will probably grow old and be just as hard to get along with."

"Don't worry. Something is about to happen in his life that will change all that. Oh, he may be provoked occasionally just as I was, but normally, he'll be a very nice old person."

"You sound as though you know him better than I do."

"I should. Let me tell you how I know."

While Harriet and M. C. Finkle were talking about the junior Finkle, Myron was seated at his desk going over yesterday's event. He picked up the old man's hat, which was still in his office, and turned it over in his hands.

"I'd better put this in the vault," he thought to himself. He rose and entered the secretary's office. She was out. The vault stood just to one side of her desk. He quickly reviewed the numbers to the combination in his head and then applied himself to the dial. There was a familiar click as the last number registered. He turned the handle and the door popped open. Inside were all the more precious holdings of the firm including files, safety deposit boxes and shelves with different paraphernalia pertaining to various inventions.

Finkle stepped into the chamber and looked around for the right place for the hat. As he did so, he placed the hat on his head thus freeing his hands to move objects aside to make room on one of the shelves.

His mind was active in another pursuit. He thought of Harriet, her father, the business and his sorry relationship in the firm.

Mostly he reflected on the old man. He wondered if he would still be the junior partner when he was that old. How would he feel?

Suddenly, the everything became a blur. It seemed that the room shifted or became something other than it was. He steadied himself against a cabinet. He felt weak.

On the shelf he had been clearing for the hat were stacks and stacks of money. He picked up a bundle.

Somehow his hands were different. They were wrinkled and the veins stood out. There were sunspots that he had never noticed before. These were not his hands. They couldn't be. They were an old man's hands.

He looked at the bills. They had funny pictures on them. They were new bills dating twenty and thirty years into the future. They were stacks of $100, $500 and $1000. Surely these were not real.

He put the stack back and picked up another one. Now this was real money. The bills in the stack were dated in his own time. They were familiar old bills. He counted the stack. In his hands he held $10,000.

"Where am I?" he thought. "Can this be real?"

As he put the money back, a pretty young lady peered into the vault. "Mr. Finkle, are you all right? Is there anything I can do for you?"

He looked up puzzled. This was not Judy, the secretary of the office.

"I'm fine," he tried to say, but the voice that came from his lips was unfamiliar. "Yes. I'm very fine," he said with a smile.

"Well, call me if you need my help." The pretty stranger left the vault. He could hear her in the outer office. She shuffled papers and opened and closed drawers. He could tell she was trying to sound busy.

Finkle's thoughts returned to the problem at hand. He thought of the things the old man had said about his stealing his money. The truth came to him strange as it seemed. The hat was magic. It had taken him to the time when he would be as old as the man who had visited his office. He had been wondering how he would feel at that age. Here he was in an old body with wrinkles. He was that old man. This was his office thirty years later. This was his vault. This was his money. He was rich.

Then, why was the old man so disturbed about his stealing from him? He looked at the money. It looked as though he would never miss much of it. If he took some of this money and returned to his own time he could buy Greathouse and Throwbridge out. How much would it take - $500, 000, a million? They were old men. They were ready to retire. They would probably welcome a buyout. Here was the way right before him.

His lips moved silently as he reflected on the possibilities: "How wonderful it would be to face those two with the means to tell them off. Life could be good with Harriet. She would never want for anything her father had."

He picked up a dusty bag that was lying in the corner. He checked the stacks one by one being careful to only take those bills minted in his time.

"But isn't this stealing?" he asked himself. "No! It couldn't be. It was his money." He counted the stacks. "How much do I have now – ten million?"

There was silence in the outer office. "May I help?"

"Oh, no, miss. I am doing quite well." Finkle adjusted the hat, picked up the bag, wished that he was young again, and thought of January 4, 2002. When things settled around him he found himself young and exuberant. His hands were young hands. He sprang from the vault and locked it. Judy, who had just returned from her break, was startled to see him.

"Oh, my, Mr. Finkle. What have you been up to in the vault?"

"Oh, I was just looking for a place for the hat."

"Well, it looks like you didn't find a place for it."

Finkle felt the brim of the hat with his free hand. "Uh, well, I cleared a place and then saw that all these old files could be thrown away. I guess I got distracted."

"May I take those to the furnace for you, Mr. Finkle?"

"No – no, I'll do it myself. I'm not an old man yet, Judy."

Finkle quickly went into his office and put the hat back on his desk. "I'm going out to the bank, Judy – err I'll drop the old files into the furnace on the way."

Finkle's trip into the future had taken less than twenty minute. While he was making his money haul to the bank, the senior Finkle and Harriet were finishing a very interesting discussion.

"So, you see Harriet, I was only trying to retrieve what I had taken from myself in this period of my life."

"What a fantastic story, Mr. Finkle. If I can believe you then, you are really my husband only thirty years older."

"Yes. That is true. A lot has happened in those thirty years to make me appreciate you, Harriet. I still work in patents and copyrights, but I don't follow the ways your father taught me. I think you would be proud of me."

"That explains how you guessed that I had brought you cinnamon dainties. Myron has always loved my cookies. I guess you still like them thirty years later."

"Actually, I miss your cookies. Harriet-er . . . you died a year ago in the plague of 2030. I miss you as well as the cinnamon dainties, Harriet." Harriet was touched by the old man's remarks. Could she believe him?

As though he anticipated her doubt, Mr. Finkle rolled up his sleeve and revealed a long red scar on his right forearm.

"Oh, my, that is Myron's saber scar! He is proud of that scar. He was wounded in college when he belonged to the fencing team." There was no question now.

"Yes. It has been with me all these years – all because of a foolish dare."

"But how did you get here? How could you come from the future?"

"It's the hat, Harriet. Twenty-five years from now I, I mean your husband will have a client with this marvelous invention. It will be a great failure because very few people can make it work. I couldn't use it at first. The man who invented it died of a broken heart.

After traveling all over the future and the past, he found he could only share it with a few. It has only been lately that I tried it again and it worked. I guess you have to be in a certain frame of mind."

"Then, there is no danger of my Myron using it. You said yourself that it didn't work for you at first."

"I have been puzzled about that. I know that I used the hat to take the cash from the vault when I was his age and I know that the money has just come up missing. Perhaps before I stole the money I was less concerned with the power of wealth, yet I was clearly after the money when I came here."

"It sounds like righteous indignation to me. You just wanted to set things straight."

"I don't know, Harriet. Is there anything such as righteous indignation?"

"I think so. Was it a lot of money that disappeared? Did it ruin your business?"

"I was devastated when it happened. I knew exactly how it happened. It hurt my finances, but its loss only slowed me down a little.

"What really hurt was my memory of the past. I mistakenly thought everything would collapse to the state where it was before I bought out your father."

"You bought out my father? Now I see how he had no further influence on you."

"It took me a while to realize that the circumstances that existed thirty years ago could not return. I have learned so much about the business that I could easily start all over without any money."

"Do you think that Myron could make it without the money or my father's help even now?"

"I'm not sure, but he, or should I say I, could never have done it without you. You are a very clever person, Harriet. I know that now. Oh, I have known it for years. I just never admitted it until you were gone."

For a moment the old man forgot that he was not talking to his dead wife. "Oh I do miss you, Harriet!"

Harriet flew into the old man's arms. "Oh, Myron, Myron, I am so sorry I died, I mean that she died. I'm so confused. You must be very lonely. Come and stay with Myron and me."

The old man gently tore himself away from Harriet. "It's no use. I must get back to my own time. I have a great many amends to make. I see clearly how I was and how I have come to be so dependent on this time of my life when I robbed my own future to get rich quick. Besides, can you see how confusing it would be to have two Myron's around the house? You know how jealous I was in my youth."

Harriet looked at the old man. Tears formed in her eyes and ran down her cheeks. She knew he was right. She wiped her eyes with his handkerchief once more and handed it back. "I'm getting your handkerchief all wet."

"I'll keep it as a sacred relic."

"That's sweet, Myron. You have become a kind gentleman."

"Oh, Harriet, I have made a big mistake. I now understand that I, I mean your husband, would never have been able to use the hat if I had not brought it here from the future. I've been such a fool. Now it's imperative that I get out of this jail and stop him from using the hat to travel into the future."

"Why, that's simple, Mr. Finkle. I will get the hat and bring it to you. Then Myron will not have a chance to use it to take your money and we can get back to a normal life."

"Oh, the money is not important. The missing money has created a little problem, but I have determined to do without it in any case. If it hadn't been taken I would never have been able to buy out my partners would I."

"That's right, but we'll stop Myron from using the hat to travel all over in time. I will get the hat!"

"Are you sure you can do it?"

"Can I make cinnamon dainties?"

"Of course. If you can make cinnamon dainties you can do anything. If you could make one more batch to take with me I would make them last a long time."

"I'll make a double batch and Myron will not be able to resist my persuasion."

Harriet was as good as her word. She baked the cookies, took some to her young husband, retrieved the hat and returned the same day.

While young Finkle was contentedly munching on cinnamon dainties and gloating over his bankbook, Harriet was bidding senior Finkle goodbye. As young Finkle was waving a cashier's check over the heads of Greathouse and Throwbridge, Harriet was giving senior Finkle a kiss and a hug. As young Finkle was admiring the new sign over the office door, senior Finkle was putting on his hat and thinking of the year 2032.

"Goodbye, Harriet!" Just as he was about to fade from view his thoughts focused on young Harriet once more. His image faded and returned several times. "Harriet, if things get bad for me can I come and visit you?"

"Of course you can. Come any time." With that the senior Finkle disappeared forever or at least for a long time.

Harriet turned around just as young Myron entered the visitor's room. "Harriet, I've been looking all over for you. The desk sergeant said you were with Mr. Finkle."

Still in a daze, Harriet smiled at her young husband. "You are wonderful, Myron."

"I am? What brought that on?" Harriet could see the image of a gray haired old man in her mind – a very gentle, soft-spoken likeness of Myron. She tilted her head back and gave Myron a big kiss.

www.ingramcontent.com/pod-product-compliance
Lightning Source LLC
Chambersburg PA
CBHW070532130626
46555CB00003B/1386